Junior High:
The *Muddle* Years

Acknowledgments

I wish to thank all those in my personal and scholastic lives who made this book possible.

Mr. Nick Productions, LLC
©2019 by Mr. Nick Productions, LLC

Edited by my longtime friend and editor/writer, Marilyn Milow Francis – Thank you

Front cover art and back cover – Kristy Klein
Book layout – Kristy Klein | seeingistudio.com

Photo of typical seventh grader – Anonymous
Published by Mr. Nick Productions, LLC ©2019

ISBN: 978-0-578-47954-5

Dedications

To Mr. K., my seventh grade New York State history teacher, whose knowledge and infectious enthusiasm rubbed off on all of us junior high pupils. And to Mr. G., my no-nonsense eighth grade grammar teacher. I learned how to compose coherent sentences because of you. But I'm not so sure if you did the reading world any favors by honing my writing skills; just sayin'.

Foreword

Those two years in junior high weren't wasted, were they? They were the best two years of my life, right? It's hard to tell; it could have gone either way.

Elementary school, with one teacher and one bathroom per classroom, ended on a positive note for me. Seventh and eighth grades, however, manifested as completely different animals. Those two wretched years were a time of transition, a time of puberty, a time of awkwardness, confusion and alienation. It was a time of having up to eight instructors daily, each with differing philosophies about teaching and life. Some were liberal, some conservative; some bombastic, some meek. It was also a time to start thinking about future possibilities while evaluating past failures and present limitations. All while trying to fit into a farm infested village full of bigoted hayseeds. At least the junior college in town mitigated the local hillbilly factor, somewhat. But my forward momentum seemed to have stalled during those two years and only my sense of humor got me through.

Hopefully this volume will expose some of those puzzling and anxious times and the levity associated with them. Although loosely based on my recollections and interpretations of actual events, this book is "technically" fictional. It is a book of humor and should be taken as such. There is no malicious intent; the only intent is to entertain!

Dr. I. Mayputz

TABLE OF CONTENTS

SEVENTH GRADE

	Introduction	xiv
1.	Rueful Recap	3
2.	All Things Buggy	6
3.	Carny Time	10
4.	A Trial Run	14
5.	The Dreaded First Day	19
6.	Tim Murphy Apologists?	22
7.	Monarch Madness	26
8.	Agriculture 101	31
9.	J. Logg	34
10.	Baseless Math	37
11.	Math Club	41
12.	The Flintlock Free Library	43
13.	The New Feminist Agenda?	45
14.	*Shag*	49
15.	The Wall	51
16.	Early Laugh Tracks	53
17.	Sighting the Sako	56
18.	More Shootin'	64
19.	Girls	68
20.	No Hoops for You!	70
21.	Padding a Future Résumé?	74

22.	Squeaky Pals	78
23.	Into the Closet	82
24.	The A.B. Affair	84
25.	Wood Chipper	87
26.	Philco Schmilco	91
27.	Home Life	96
28.	Scholastic Scope	99
29.	Those Blasted Ivories	102
30.	Wrastlin'	105
31.	Hobbies and Passions	109
32.	War	112
33.	Entertaining Sports	114
34.	Ski Bums?	118
35.	The Victory Garden?	122
36.	Vietnam	127
37.	Bats in the Belfry?	132
38.	Creamy Goodness	136
39.	The Biking Caravan	139
40.	The Yorker Club	142
41.	Artistically Declined	146
42.	Expectations	150
43.	Uncomfortably Dumb	156

44. Starting Anew   163
45. Silly Putty and PEZ   164
46. The "Lost" Summers   165
47. Second Helping   172
48. Still Flailing in Math!   174
49. Conjugate This....   179
50. The Silver Cap   182
51. The Hard Way   188
52. Westward Ho!   191
53. Explosive Science   196
54. Stringing Us Along   200
55. Study Halls   204
56. Smoking in the Boys' Room   207
57. Dad's Job   209
58. Mispronunciations   213
59. To Your Health!   217
60. Metallurgy 101   220
61. Alpine English   226
62. The Little Theatre   229
63. "Say Something Nice?"   231
64. Still Athletically Inclined   234
65. That Damn Duffle Bag   238
66. A New Standard   244
67. The "Gang's" Formation   246

68.	Gone Sailing	249
69.	Townies vs. Techies	252
70.	Fixtures	256
71.	I'm Not Liberace!	259
72.	Malevolent Music	261
73.	An Old Hand	265
74.	Whatever Happened to Dusty?	268
75.	ZotZ	270
76.	Guidance?	273
77.	Specs	276
78.	The Broken Pinky	278
79.	Up to Speed	282
80.	Jarts and Friends	286
81.	Disclaimer	291
82.	Last Words	293
	About the Author	296

Introduction

This book is a slightly fictionalized account of my life in junior high school, the "lost" years, inspired by actual events. Embellishments of strange happenings were unnecessary because human foibles ran rampant. However, most names and places have been altered so as not to embarrass the guilty, inept and downright scurvy. The stories are retold in a series of vignettes which best captured my mood at the time. Troubling, boring, exasperating and anxiety-ridden; I believe those adjectives accurately summed up my junior high experience. For me, seventh and eighth grades in a rural village school system were difficult to negotiate and to get a firm grip on. I had prospered in elementary school, with high school looming on the horizon. But those two intervening grades flummoxed and aggravated me. I managed to stumble and *muddle* through them and just barely escaped, mostly sane I think. Anyway, I couldn't help but write down some of my humorous misadventures that unwittingly occurred along the way. Hopefully you will laugh along with me. Maybe at me, as well!

Enjoy.

Dr. I. Mayputz

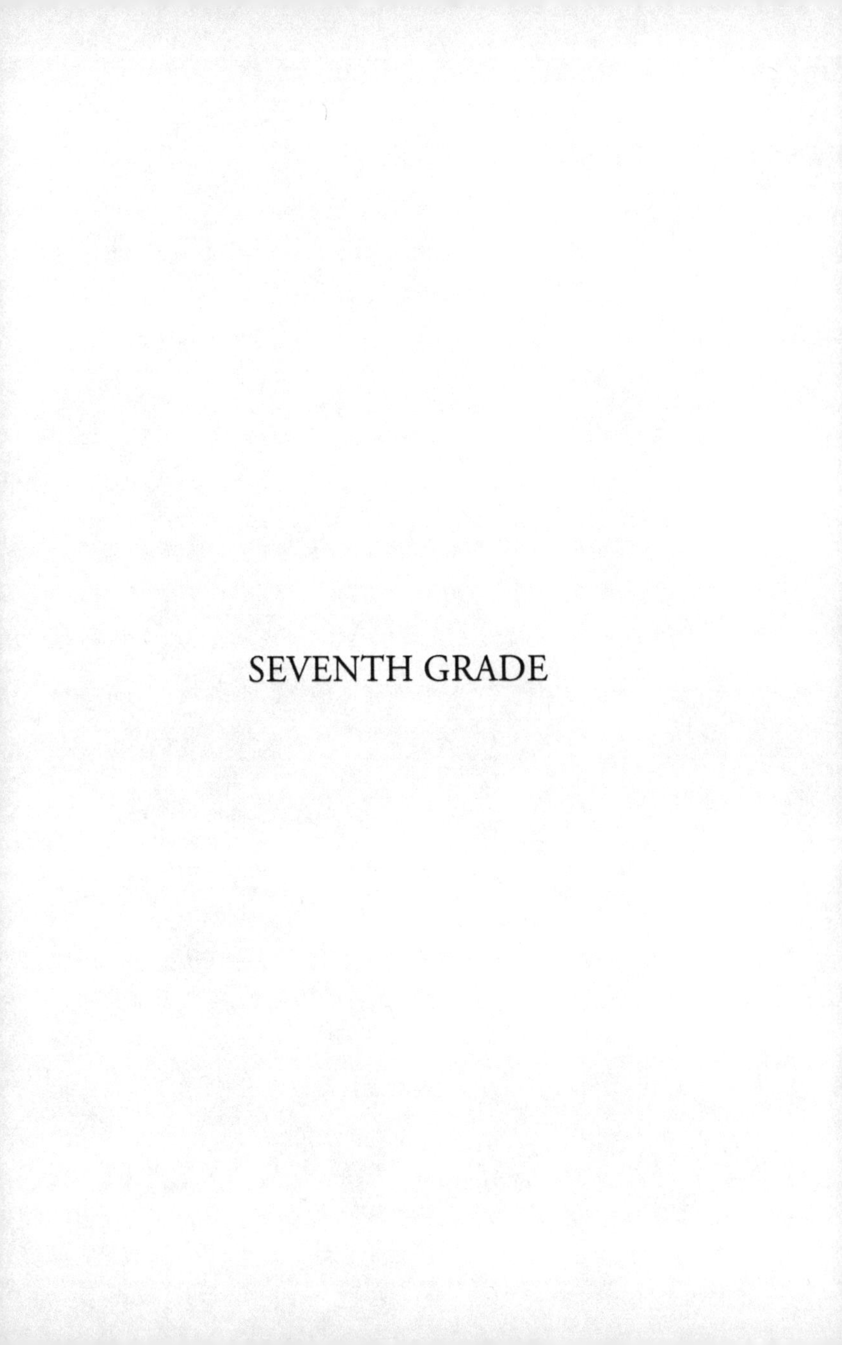

SEVENTH GRADE

Rueful Recap

To all the genuinely enthusiastic readers out there, as well as the faux bookworms faking enthusiasm, a brief background story is vital before we embark on a comedic and wordy romp through this volume. No one wants to jump into junior high school without at least knowing some salient facts about the chicanery and misadventures that transpired in grades K-6. Although a book has already been written about my elementary school life and that so-called *educational* era, here is a very short synopsis thereof: I was born in a western New York State industrialized and dirty metropolis, to accent-laden, Estonian immigrant parents. Pop hated his job and took a teaching gig as a civil engineering professor at a junior college in the Catskills, just before I started kindergarten. We moved from the familiar haunts of a multicultural and diversity enlightened city to the prejudiced and bigoted, country bumpkin, farmland/wasteland of southeastern New York State. A skinny, black-haired and brown-skinned American lad went from fitting in beautifully to becoming an outsider, a "foreigner," desperately looking to blend into a sea of blonde hair and blue-eyed interbred local yokel

spawn in a dusty and tiny no-account settlement with one
traffic light and a puny, public school system. Sure, the
town vaunted an NJCAA college, but the redneck village
idiots were ubiquitous and interactions with them became
necessary evils. And, it seems that there were bovines
everywhere, some colored black-and-white and others
brown. Curious cattle routinely cozied up to the barbwire
fence bordering our back yard just to say hello. However, at
the beginning, I didn't know one type of cow from another.
Our new village boasted dozens of small, family-run dairy
farms, mostly pumping stations for exporting milk. Our
county was known as the second highest producer of milk
and milk products in the entire state. Because my mother
was a stay-at-home housewife at the time and my father
was insulated in his cloistered community of collegial
thinkers up on the hill, I was the one that took a "beating"
as the proverbial new "black" kid in town in the early '60s
and, in the early *daze* of grammar school classes, which I
took with the mostly tow-headed and pale faced natives.
Holy hell, it was brutal at times. But I survived and
thrived, thanks to an ounce of brain, many open-minded
teachers, a few friendly neighbors, chucklehead pals of
mine, and my growing sense of humor. Of course, having a
relatively thick skin – it was already brown – helped
enormously. I was raised as a free-range child and my

youthful passions lay in naturalistic and zoological pursuits, sports – namely tennis – and science. Slightly more than one hundred original boys and girls began our educational journey together, first in the separate elementary school and then moving into the large main building down the hill, for grades 4-12. Then there were additions and deletions to the student body as time went along. Most of the seventh and eighth grade classes would be held on the second floor of our grand high school; somehow, we neophyte nitwits would have to fit together without mangling each other in the hallways between class periods. I managed to sanely navigate through elementary school (K-6) with many school friends in tow and looked forward to more "education" in junior high, in addition to learning all I could about the dairy industry and cattle varieties, just to be on the safe side, in case I had an emergency and HAD to interact with a local, shit-stomping, hick.

2

All Things Buggy

Ah, the summer of '71. Woodstock had already "happened," my professor father was getting ready to depart for the first leg of summer school at RIT to eventually earn a master's degree (though he would be back in time for our annual, two-week, August camping trip), our dead-end street was brutally ripped up as the next roadway to have septic pipes laid in it to connect to our homes, and I was content to shirk my workaholic paternal grandfather to catch insects, salamanders, and the like. I thought it would be a great summer also filled with tennis, swimming, fishing and bike riding. I was eleven, had successfully made it out of elementary school and eagerly embraced the time off. Rarely bored, I had things to do, places to explore; I was a little boy constantly in motion, physically and mentally. Roughly two minutes away, and down a steep hill, I was allowed to visit Clinton street, the old and familiar road where I grew up, as well as the faithful, creepy-crawly-filled brook behind the grand Victorian houses that lined that treed boulevard. And I still stopped in periodically to visit Dr. C. R., a retired Presbyterian pastor and amateur entomologist who took me on as a *special pupil* when I was seven-years-old. I was ready for another joyous summer, but summer was not ready for me. As a relatively pessimistic optimist, I hated change and relished continuity of life, especially if it was fun-filled and productive for me. I looked forward to new "things" but at the same time wanted certain "things" to stay the same. Well, my father left, I had no one to play tennis with, couldn't go bike riding because the village sewer system project made our narrow street a big mess, and my beloved brook exploded and flooded our village because of an unforeseen rainy deluge. On top of that, my grandfather thought he should over-parent me, fishing was out, and my sister started to really annoy me. All I had left was swimming, hitting tennis balls against a concrete wall at the nearby college and my "bugs" to keep me sane and satisfied. What a shitty summer it was turning out to be! First and foremost, I had to plan daily how to outsmart, outfox and outwit my sister and Grandpa Pete. It seemed that both wanted a piece of me during my waking hours. Sis wanted me to play with her and my task-oriented and work-obsessed Estonian grandpa wanted nothing more than to keep me home to forcibly "teach" me responsibility: how to work hard from morning till night at "manly" jobs to get that zoological crap out of my head. It was for my own good he would lecture. Now, mind you, we lived on a quarter-acre of land, in town, had a beautiful new house, had all the modern bells and whistles of the '70s and here was Grandpa Pete still psychologically living like an Estonian farmer, and trying to convert me to being one, as well. No way, Jose'! Come on, I had heard a few licks of Led Zeppelin, man! The music, our nation, and I were slowly losing our country roots and innocence. Now, I didn't mind picking stones out of our large garden once in a while, or helping him change the oil and filter in one of our cars, but I never bought into his wholesale, old-fashioned work ethos. He would literally "find" work to do! And my younger sister couldn't keep depending on me for entertainment. What did I look like, her personal clown? My mom was a homemaker, she had no outside job, and she was responsible for my sibling, not me. So, I had to craftily and cleverly find ways to "disappear" if I wanted to pursue my derelict hobbies, as my grandfather put it. My father, although not a fan of my "addictions," was nonetheless a buffer for me as well as a fellow tennis player, coach, and fisherman. Now he was gone for at least three months. Mom knew I had to get out of that dour household as often as possible and usually she facilitated my escapes. She was also not always a fan of her father-in-law. Thanks, mom. I took solace during those warm months mainly in all things buggy and begrudgingly looked forward to school again in the fall. But I would be a seventh-grader now and the anxiety was starting to build in me. I had received my upcoming school schedule and my old man would be home soon, just in time for our camping trip. I had managed to keep that maniacal work horse called Grandpa Pete at bay and gone swimming with my pals at the village pool numerous times. I had even played with my sister on occasion. I hated change but changed myself during that event-filled summer. I was growing up, I guess. Life was starting to throw me curveballs, but I hit a few. And puberty was just around the corner....

3

Carny Time

The summer of '71 was fast ending and I was glad. My professor father would be back from his summer-school stint at RIT and I would officially be in junior high. And I would finally get my grandpa Pete off my back! But there was something curious about my paternal grandfather. Although a gruff and old world tough guy with a work ethic second to none, he nonetheless made a point to "relax" daily with power naps and the occasional levity that HE deemed as wholesome fun and entertaining. If HE sanctioned it, then it was alright to indulge in; if I or other family members tried to initiate a humorous outburst or outing, he frowned and admonished us for our wanton frivolity and alleged decadence. For instance, watching *Sanford and Son*, *All in the Family* and *Abbott and Costello* on TV were righteous endeavors but viewing "trash" such as *I Dream of Jeannie* and *Gilligan's Island* were not. Going out on the town at night was a no-no, but catching the annual carnival at Legion Field, just outside of the village, was considered good, clean fun. The carnival experience reminded me of many TV Westerns that I had already watched; the cowboys worked like dogs for months, uncomplaining and sweat soaked, only to be rewarded by the upcoming hoedown in a local hamlet where they would get drunk and go wild with the ladies for a brief time. Then, back to work as usual. Was that how my grandfather's life had been in rural Estonia when he was growing up as a youth: unrelenting and tedious daily labor with the occasional wilding? He was now living in America (for the last twenty-five years, no less), where "fun" was to be had every day! What was wrong with him? That work-related piety of his was really grating on me and I rebelled at every chance. But now the carnival was coming to town and at least Grandpa Pete approved of it. I guess we would go, after all. This was a yearly extravaganza for our dinky town and lots of the plain folks were rightfully excited about it. A carnival! The hype pitched to the locals was astounding: three tents, a semi circus, games galore, and rides to fill a football field. What a bonanza! The slick and colorful bills put up around town promised a three-day, glorious, inexpensive and fantastic experience. It was as if a charismatic evangelist was coming to liberate the inbred local "losers" from the supposed doldrums and stupor they were in. I agree that the masses were asses, but even I could hardly wait. This was going to be my first time. Carny time! Well, you can guess the rest of the story. There was only one tent set up, the rides were all rusty and paltry in number, the mangy animals were just barely breathing, and the hosts were dirty, disheveled outliers that parents always warned their children not to become. Never marry an actor/actress or join the circus! At least that's what I heard in my home on numerous occasions. We went for one day only, at dusk. My sister, mom, grandfather and I took in the sights, sounds and smells on that large muddy field. Nevertheless, I quickly realized that I was above that kind of lark, but, there stood Grandpa Pete, smiling, pointing and laughing as if finally quaffing a long, overdue quenching drink as a reward for his stoic and no-frills, toiling, lifestyle. I was sickened at the sight. THAT is what made him happy and lighthearted? A bunch of drunken and dismal con artist carnies barely going through the motions to entertain the equally drab and hobo-resembling natives? Sad is what it was. I did not enjoy myself, unlike most of the gawking and cotton candy-covered townspeople all around me. What was wrong with me? What was wrong with them? However, I DID take some pleasure in aping the caged monkeys while nibbling on a sugary, sweet, powdered, funnel cake. But I didn't win any of the rigged ring tosses or dastardly dart games and couldn't secure my sister anything larger than a cheap plastic whistle. The rides were old, creaky, and scary. We didn't return for the next two nights. However, my grandpa and most of the large crowd crowed about the event for weeks; I just wanted to forget it. But at least we HAD been to an "official" circus and I DID sit inside a canvas big top and ate stale and salty popcorn, while watching the "drugged up" and obviously docile lions "be tamed." It had been a flea-bitten experience and I correctly surmised that we would be back again the following summer, if THEY showed up again. Was I slowly dumbing down and turning into a numbskull native? My grades had been top notch all through grammar school but was I psychologically getting damaged and going down the toilet? I hoped not. Pop was coming home soon and, besides playing tennis again, I would go huntin' and fishin' with him. Uh oh, perhaps this village living WAS starting to rub off on me? But I had hated that bullshit carnival adventure, so I guessed I was still alright in the head! For now.

4

A Trial Run

It was a few days before seventh grade began in earnest; my family and I had just arrived back from our "mandatory," annual, oceanside, camping trip to Connecticut and I was getting my thoughts together for the upcoming school year. I also deftly rearranged my jars full of monarch butterfly caterpillars and praying mantids that I kept on the porch. I went upstairs, stared at my class schedule, looked at my required pencils, pens, and notebooks strewn haphazardly on my bed and exhaled deeply as I tried to remember all the details that Paul F. had emphatically told me about before I finished sixth grade. I lay back on my bed, closed my eyes and tried hard not to panic. Toward the end of the sixth-grade year, each rising seventh grader was given a day off to shadow a real seventh grader for the entire day, going to all of her/his classes, eating lunch with her/him and getting the "feel" of high school. Kind of like a trial run before the REAL educational commotion commenced. Paul F. was assigned to be my big brother that day. I sort of knew him through family connections as a short, unpopular, dweeby kid with a nervous disposition. I didn't care about his personal quirks and was quite excited

as he stopped by my classroom right after morning
announcements to pick me up for the day's scholastic
activities. This was going to be fun, I thought. I would be
tagging along an upperclassman all day long with no
worries, no classroom assignments to fulfill, and no
homework to do at night. Bring it on. Paul and I shook
hands as my teacher nodded at both of us and, off we
went. First stop: the second floor! Chattering all the way
up the marble stairs, Paul talked nonstop as I was
eyeballing the madhouse in front of me. Kids were
everywhere, the noise level deafening, with Paul yelling
into my face to keep up and not hold him back. We raced
to his locker and he expertly spun the combination lock to
open it. He grabbed some books and notepads, slammed
the gray metal door shut and began a slow jog to his first
class: math! There were only four minutes available
between periods, so no dawdling was allowed. I easily kept
up and soon we were seated as my future math teacher
started her futile spiel. No one seemed to notice me or Paul
for that matter. Nobody talked to him, either. I surmised
that although somewhat of a character, he was not exactly
well liked. No worries, though. This went on all morning,
with me seated by his side and listening to different
teachers spew their stuff. In between classes we did the
same old locker routine, kind of like a pit stop to get fresh

tires and adjust the track bar, and then burned rubber to
arrive at the next classroom on time. You had to be in
shape though. Four minutes seemed barely enough time to
get your shit together or, take one, before the upcoming
lecture. But Paul was a pro; he wasn't even winded while
traversing the packed and raucous hallway from one end to
the other. Then it was lunchtime and a much needed pee
break, for me. I don't know when HE went, if he went at
all. Maybe he had a giant bladder? A.W., the checkout
lunch lady, the one with the glasses, piled up hair and
chewing gum-snapping habit, smiled when she recognized
me. Her husband was my sometime bus driver and we all
knew each other. She punched me out, my meal ticket that
is, and Paul and I sat together to chow down. We ate
alone, no one sat next to us. Paul wasn't upset or dissolute,
he just kept yakking away as if having no friends was his
lot in life and nothing to be depressed about. And forget
about girls. I was the one that kept looking around to see if
we were being stared at or made fun of from a distance.
Nothing. Everyone was seated in groups or twosomes and
noisily munched away as Paul continued his blabbering.
Once in a while, he mentioned something worthwhile and
got my attention but for the most part it was useless and
monotonous gibberish that kept coming out of his cake-
hole. Oh, well, at least it was nice of him to have

volunteered to do this job. I guess I appreciated it, reluctantly, of course. It's funny but I didn't see any other sixth graders with their "guides," but then, I wasn't actively searching them out either. Lunch period ended, and the dizzying afternoon stopped after art class, and Paul walked me back to my sixth-grade classroom. He had early dismissal on Thursdays and Fridays and could leave before 3 o'clock while we elementary grunts had to stay until 3:06 p.m., before we ran for our buses. It had been a maddening day and I barely remembered anything that Paul or the various seventh-grade teachers had uttered. As I laid there in my own bed with my eyes still tightly shut, I recollected the crowded hallway, the cigarette smoke-filled bathrooms, the combination lock numbers on the locker that had to be memorized, the hectic pushing, shoving, touching, and grabbing that occurred every time the damn bell rang, and the shear anxiety of it all. Could I handle it? I had to, I was growing up; I couldn't backslide now, plus my grades were too high. I was going up the steps into seventh grade and junior high whether I liked it or not. However, I would be in regular instead of advanced math and would continue with piano, tennis, table tennis, and a new artistic hobby, the violin. I had started violin lessons while in sixth grade and would now be part of the high school orchestra. I don't know why I picked it up because, unlike piano, I sucked at

It. However some of my close pals were also inept at their respective musical instruments, but they kept at it. So, I did too. Plus, maybe the orchestral rehearsals during school hours would be fun while surrounded by my chums? And it turned out to be so. I slowly opened my eyes, stared at my mimeographed, blue, schedule in my hand and hoped for the best. Paul F. had formerly blurted out lots of nonsense but one thing did resonate with me: "Putz," he had stammered, "You have to be *cool* if you want to survive." Was he *cool* and nobody knew it? Was I *cool*? I would soon find out.

5

The Dreaded First Day

This was it, the first day of class. Grammar school had finished finishing us and most of we plebes were moving on into junior high, seventh grade, that is. It was a bold step, a necessary step, a *fresh step* in my educational endeavors. And it was way too late to be anxious. All my worrying during the previous summer vacation had not erased the inevitable for me. The day dawned early and was upon me in no time. I said goodbye to my younger sister and rapidly departed Bus 57, which was parked and percolating in front of the familiar Big House, MY high school. Grades four through six were taught in a separate wing in that very building so I was very well acquainted with the layout. The bus finally rumbled away to discharge the remaining little tykes into the separate K-3 elementary school building, where sis was still a prisoner. Meanwhile, I bounded up the granite steps, and bolted through the enormous open front doors into the foyer and nervously looked about at the madhouse I had involuntarily joined. I suddenly realized that I had forgotten what I had eaten for breakfast, or even what day it was. I was in a *daze*. I stared down at my feet to make sure my socks matched. They did, both were blue, at least. Okay, time to manage the butterflies in my stomach and go find my second-floor locker. The numbering was in bold black print and I found it alright, but there was a behemoth of a student standing in front of it and blocking my way. What the hell? Then I remembered that we would be sharing a locker in junior high; that was the rule. And we had no choice of locker mate, at least not at first. I checked my watch and realized that we had to be in our assigned homeroom in less than three minutes and this moron was still diddling with the combination and appeared stressed and sweaty. But I sort of knew him; we had spoken on the playground here and there. I thought he was a decent fellow. But now he was swearing and bellowing at the lock and denting the door from numerous, frustrated fist blows. I quickly interjected. He had not seen me that whole time and recoiled for a brief instance, fortuitously allowing me to adeptly spin the lock and open the locker door. We both unceremoniously dumped our coats, hats and notebooks into the dark recess but not before J. Logg harshly reminded me that HE would get the top "bunk" in the locker and not me. Snarling and spitting as he slammed the door shut, he took off, at least as fast as a skinny-challenged kid of his size could move. I stood there for a moment to reflect on what had just happened. There was no need for him to have been so testy and brusque. Didn't he recognize or remember me? Was he also agitated, or had I grossly misjudged him as a potential future pal? Then I literally ran into my nearby homeroom and took an empty seat against the blackboard. Other kids were tardy but kindly Mrs. N. understood. It was the first freakin' day! Mrs. N. would turn out to be one of my favorite teachers in high school, teaching ninth grade English; I liked her already. Morning announcements commenced with the familiar sounding, gravelly baritone voice emanating from the loudspeaker on the wall. Principal S. welcomed the whole high school and went on and on about a new year, etc. However, I was still deep in thought about J. Logg, my locker mate. This initial animosity between us would not do but how could I hurriedly fix it? Class attendance was taken as I peered at the familiar herd all around me; I had known most of my fellow *cretins* since kindergarten. We all looked scared, like wide-eyed wildebeests about to encounter preying lions. The bell rang and I ran out into the hall and before long was seated in New York State history, my first class of the day. On the way there I had wisely bypassed my locker but glanced anyway to see that familiar, surly, mass, standing there, again in a bewildered state while fiddling with the combination. Was J. Logg really a numerical numbnuts? How was I going to put up with this crap for eight periods a day, and for a year? How, indeed?

6

Tim Murphy Apologists?

There was no alphabetical seating in that class as we greenhorns sat wherever we wanted. I quickly grabbed a desk against the far wall in the middle of the row. I anxiously waited for the stern looking, tall, exceedingly handsome, very young, bespectacled, teacher to say something. And say something he did, or should I say he orated for close to twenty minutes, non-stop! After we *schlubs* had quieted down, Mr. K. proceeded to introduce himself and the subject he was going to teach us: seventh grade New York State history. He was from a friendly neighboring county and, this was his initial year teaching at our school, and OUR first year learning historical factoids about the Empire State. It seemed we were both new at this game. But before we could act out or *86* his efforts, he took the initiative and boldly wrote his last name on the blackboard in huge block letters, while simultaneously yelling out each letter at the top of his lungs. His surname rhymed with the word cruiser and he took great pains in having us learn the correct spelling of his family name, or else. He wasn't mean, he just cleverly knew how to effectively take control of a classroom full of

rambunctious twelve-year-olds. And he also had the
wisdom to describe an interesting year-long curriculum
that he had planned. For many, it was love at first sight as
he commenced to instruct us. The girls giggled and
blushed demurely as he seductively sashayed around the
room and the guys instantly became gung-ho adherents of
his infectious and passionate teaching methods. Although a
hard marker and the purveyor of difficult exam questions,
none of us took it out on him, blaming ourselves for our
gross ineptitude, and embarrassed for not pleasing him. He
had us in the palm of his hand and even I looked forward
to that class every day, and the frequent projects that we
had to accomplish for that man. I recall having fabricated
accurate Haudenosaunee (Iroquois) Indian long house
miniatures, complete with beech tree bark and twine,
which he appreciatively kept in his classroom for decades,
long after my graduation. He covered all aspects of
prehistoric and ancient New York State, up to the present
times. However, his favorite time period was the American
Revolutionary War, the one that the French got involved in
only after the organized colonial combatants bravely
showed that they could fight and win. And because the war
factually turned in the militiamen's favor during the Battles
of Saratoga in upstate New York, Mr. K. waxed nostalgic
about the glorious details of those specific hostilities and

their ramifications. And then there was his idolized war hero, Timothy Murphy. Mr. Murphy, a second-generation Irishman born at the Delaware river basin border of Pennsylvania and New Jersey, was the most famous military marksman of his time. As an army sergeant/rifleman, he reputedly killed British General Simon Fraser and his attache', Sir Francis Drake, during the second battle of Saratoga, the battle of Bemis Heights. It seems that just as Fraser and Drake were rallying the English regulars, Murphy allegedly took them out in succession from at least a distance of 300 yards. But, were his patriotic exploits on that day only a myth and unprovable hyperbolic folklore? It was the turning point in the war, you know, so these things historically mattered. Supposedly, there were at least twelve snipers ordered to do the dirty work, yet Murphy got the everlasting legendary credit. Some witnesses swore he was the triggerman, some doubted it. He himself didn't deny that he could have been the responsible party. Since most of the stories about him were indeed documented as true, even latter-day history scholars had difficulty parsing the probable bits of fiction and unintentional hype that were most likely woven into the rich Murphy lexicon. As relatively gullible seventh grade goobers, already smitten by our charismatic teacher, it was a cinch for us to accept the classroom speechifying as gospel; we listened in awed rapture while Mr. K. made "Timothy Murphy" believers out of us. After other skirmishes and the end of the revolution, Mr. Murphy sired 13 children with two successive wives, retired to Charlotteville, N.Y., and is buried in Middleburg, N.Y., where a bronze plaque proudly proclaims him a hero of Schoharie county. Anyhow, we did learn quite a lot more history than just about the Revolutionary War, but Timothy Murphy kept popping up periodically as Mr. K.'s shining example of manly fortitude, righteousness and virtuous zealotry. The scholastic year went by smoothly although the exams never became easier. Nevertheless, we persevered and took our lumps in the grading department, but, couldn't care less. It had been an honor to be taught by someone with Mr. K's enthusiasm, and at the end we were saddened to say goodbye to a good man and a great teacher. Thanks, Ed.

7

Monarch Madness

Oh, joy, seventh-grade Life Science class! I had literally run into that room and quickly found a front row berth. I sat down, looked up and fell backward in my hard, wooden seat. There, at the front of the room, behind a black laboratory desk with a black marble countertop sat a stooped, bespectacled, gray-haired and very elderly, genuine, African-American gentleman – our teacher. He had craggy lines on his weathered face and deep crow's feet by his eyes. And, hey, he was darker than me! I instantly hoped that my fellow classmates would take notice and strike me from their memory banks as a "black" kid. This guy was the real McCoy, but what was he doing here anyway? He was the only real black person in the entire school. Surely, he had felt and witnessed years of racism and blatant discrimination in our basically "all white," one horse town? I was only here for a short while and already felt the brunt of inappropriate comments and negativity about my surname and the color of MY skin and hair. This guy was old and must have endured similar torments for years. How could he have taken it? Why was he still here? How did he fit into the smoke-filled teacher's lounge during breaks? Was he a local, and a *token* teacher for diversity's sake; in THAT biased era? I never got any answers to those thought-provoking questions because they were only in my mind. I never asked them out loud! I was still slightly puzzled as I quieted my pea brain and settled down for a bout of science from that man. I had heard rumors that he was a decent instructor and he was, right from the beginning. We cracked open our textbooks to chapter one as Mr. V.N. sat there, unmoving, clearing his throat. He was a stoic, unsmiling and deliberate orator, obviously conditioned by a lifetime of teaching young nincompoops about a "dry" subject such as SCIENCE! He had a strict and stern approach to learning as we soon found out. He wasn't mean, just thorough and dogmatic. No one in the class moved a muscle. Even the boisterous farm boys sat still, staring straight ahead without flinching. Maybe he had more energy and enthusiasm as a young lecturer and now simply went through the motions, but they were good motions, and I was learning a lot from this old timer. Every class period, after mandatory roll call, we were obliged to read the following book chapter, a paragraph apiece, round and round the room until the chapter was finished. He would point a gnarled index finger at each of us in turn, announce our names and implore us to start reading where the previous student had left off. He didn't trust us to read at home and basically gave us a head start on the next day's material. Of course, I reread the same chapter at home nightly just to be on the safe side and because I truly relished the subject matter. Anyhow, after our reading session, he would slowly extricate himself from behind his lab counter and launch into the present day's subject, writing copious notes on the blackboard as well as explaining photosynthesis, biological principles, animal life cycles, etc. I loved it all. Other classmates, not so much. To each their own, however. One early fall Monday, on a whim, I brought in a few of my large glass jars full of Monarch butterfly caterpillars that I was rearing that late summer and, plopped down my goods on a vacant wooden table at the front of the room. Some specimens were still larvae, chewing up milkweed leaves and pooping like crazy, some were already in the crysalid form, ready to hatch in a few weeks time. As a well-known junior amateur naturalist among my immediate peeps and neighbors, it was a no-brainer for me, and fellow students gathered around my display and nodded in unison that that's just what I did. Some lingered to closely observe the antennaed black and white caterpillars munching away. Mr. V.N. quickly hobbled over to the display with an astonished look on his face. His uninspiring and dour expression lifted, and he immediately started to grin from ear to ear and proceeded to compliment me on my *chutzpah* and initiative for bringing in some live and lively life forms to his classroom for discussion. He kept staring at me in disbelief as other students reassured him that it was all quite *kosher* and normal for me. I had had a "buggy" reputation since kindergarten and what I brought in was in keeping with my passion. He still couldn't believe it. A kid in his lackluster and stuffy class had livened things up with squiggly and wriggly caterpillars? It couldn't be, or, could it? Pupils stood around and discussed my mini menagerie and seemed scientifically inspired by the short and impromptu show-and-tell discourse. Once we were all seated, Mr. N. breathlessly told us that we would deviate from the next chapter and focus on metamorphosis, thanks to my collection. He outlined some future chapters to read and began a dialogue on insects, cocoons, butterflies and moths. I sat there like a proud male peacock, while learning about something that I already knew. It was also nice to see Mr. N. act like a young man again, excited about teaching and investigating animals that were placed right in front of him. I think I gave him a jolt that late September and he appreciated it. It was all old hat to me but he didn't know it, as I nonchalantly explained things to my classmates as a seasoned insect lover. It was an autumn to remember and I'll never forget that class, old Mr. N., and his *old school* teaching ways. What started out as a boring and niggardly class, devoid of "life," with a niggling teacher, ended up a great introductory science course. I eased into an easy A average at year's end and had Mr. N. to thank for it. He stuck to his science guns and taught willing AND unwilling students alike the basic tenets of biological science. I miss him.

8

Agriculture 101

The first day of school, sullied by my bellicose and portly locker mate and all the expected hustle-bustle of a busy second floor in my pastoral high school, seemed blissfully over. Now it was eighth period and time for the last class of the day, the course I had been dreading: Agriculture. It was a mandatory, male only, quarterly course for seventh and eighth graders in our boondocks school. I HAD to take it; it was required! While all the girls took two quarters of home economics from that *hot* teacher Mrs. D., we boys had to take both Ag. and Wood Shop before journeying into successive quarters of coed music and art while in junior high. That's how it was back then. Since we were a rural, dairy producing area in "Bumfuck," N.Y., it all made sense, at least to the administration and the myriad of farm family students enrolled in the high school. The local two-year college professors' progeny, of which I was one, suffered the same fate and had to take it on the chin and on the report card to successfully graduate from our "esteemed" but often countrified, Roman-columned, place of *larnin'*. I entered the bus garage building, found the class door for that "farm" course, and settled down in a front

row seat very close to the blackboard. Since I was
functionally nearsighted, I put on my prescription specs
just in case and got ready for the beef. Wait a minute. I
didn't know a Jersey from a Guernsey cow, darn it. (That's a
Guernsey on the front cover, by the way). I was doomed.
At least I could identify a black-and-white Holstein. So, all
was not lost. But farming practices, types of feed,
horticulture, agriculture, aquaculture and hydroponics?
Did Mr. F. say, "Fun with phonics?" Help! Fortunately, we
were issued detailed and photo-enhanced textbooks. And
within a relatively short period of time I was acing the class
exams and also asking rather intelligent questions. While
the disruptive, farm-boy herd in the back of the class
hooted, hollered and were "busy" fooling around, those of
us that read the course book and listened in class actually
learned somethin'. I ended up with the highest classroom
average, but the teacher wasn't surprised. However,
whenever he had admonished that "wild bunch" in the
back rows for low test grades, they didn't seem to care.
They were all poised to inherit their daddy's farms one day
and basically already knew the rudiments of running them.
Those arrogant, John Deere capped chaps, with calloused
hands from milking, obviously thought that they knew it
all and would be all set, for life. And they were most likely
correct. I was the nervous Nellie that was just grateful for

getting through that class. With A's of course, but still.…
And now I could be confident if threatened to converse
with a local lout about udder rashes or how much DDT to
spray on a corn crop. By the way, the vaunted DDT
pesticide that was widely used to eliminate pestilence
wasn't banned until 1972. But wait another minute.… The
scholastic quarter ended, I rejoiced, but was reminded by
Mr. F. that another helping of Agriculture would
commence next fall in eighth grade, with more of the
same: alfalfa sprouts, bovines, cornpone and buckwheat
bullshit. Help!

9

J. Logg

Why devote a section of this book to that recalcitrant, sometime incorrigible and loudmouthed brute? Because I had to. Hear me out, please. It was bad enough that I was forced to share a teeny-weeny locker with another boy, but that boy/man was a "belligerent bully," with a peach fuzz, black mustache under his nose. To make matters worse, the entire school was recently shellacked, you know, all the classroom hardwood floors were polyurethane lacquered prior to the school opening. And the stench was horrible, at least to me. That unmistakable *stank* reminded me of each prior first week of school and my associated high levels of anxiety. I hated it. Olfactory mnemonics are a bitch! Anyhow, back to J. Logg. Our only point of contact was at that darn gray locker; we had no classes together, not even homeroom. He was on a non Regents business track; I, on a science/math trajectory, with college and post graduate degrees hopefully in my future. We sat with different sets of friends during the midday chowtime. He was big and relatively ungainly; I was skinny, wiry and athletic. Between class periods, we looked like Tennessee Tuxedo and Chumley while huddling next to our narrow locker door opening. We seemed to have NOTHING in common but a few funny stories and fellow character assassinations that we regularly chuckled about. Nevertheless, what began as outright animosity and frequent angry outbursts, on his part, slowly dissipated into a tepid truce and genuine camaraderie, followed by a lifelong solid friendship. Numerous play dates at our respective homes, punctuated by loads of laughter and inside jokes, punctured our former disdain for each other. He became an intimate and stalwart member of our future "gang" of like-minded female/male jokesters that started to foment and ferment by the end of seventh grade. J. Logg's savvy, business-minded family owned our one and only Getty gasoline/"convenience" shop, called Logg's Store, on upper Main Street, at the outskirts of town. It was ahead of its time, closing at 11 p.m. weekdays and way past midnight on weekends, whereas the local Grand Union and Victory marts shut down at 6 p.m. That overstocked but miniscule fuel/food emporium was attached to their home. The Loggs made a good living, especially during the late evening hours, selling "everything" from Colt 45 malt liquor to Chef Boyardee canned ravioli to the local villagers and college students in town. It was tactically smart for a long time, until the village supermarkets wised up and stayed open later. His family was jovial and eclectic, always urging me to eat raw celery stalks, like they did, whenever I visited and ate meals at his house. He started out as a slightly tubby, acne-ridden, willful adolescent but somehow glommed on to we *cool* wisenheimers early on in the game. And I'm grateful he did. He became a trusted confidante, and frequent "go-to" guy. Was all this due to cohabiting an unremarkable locker with me? Perhaps? Probably. Because although I was a relatively unremarkable, dark-skinned, *wiseguy* at the time, I supposedly had PO-tential, and liked to make people laugh, as did he. Maybe we had much more in common than our disparate scholastic and athletic endeavors would indicate? I guessed so! However, why the rough beginning betwixt us? I don't know, I never asked him for an explanation. Nevertheless, nearly fifty years later, he is still a close friend.

10

Baseless Math

While it was painfully obvious that I did not possess the textbook numerical reasoning power of some of my smart friends, I did seem to understand most arithmetical concepts. Or, so I thought. Nevertheless, I found myself in the regular seventh-grade math class, instead of the advanced one that most of my pals were in. So, things should have been easy for me, right? Even my frequently disappointed and math wizard father seemed to think so. Not so fast, not so fast! I entered Mrs. H.'s classroom with a bitterly bad attitude for seemingly having been slighted and "demoted" to the dummy section and thought I could just wing it. I was supposedly smart, remember? Yeah, a smart-aleck but not a math whiz! Oh, boy. We were seated in alphabetical order and of course, with my near-sightedness, I sat in the last seat in my row, as far away from the blackboard as possible. I had glasses but didn't always wear them. They probably needed a new correction at that point, but I just didn't care. I mean, how hard could this math be? Mrs. H., the mother of a fellow female student, was middle-aged and spoke in soft measured tones and tried to peddle math as an exciting topic. Yeah, right.

She reassuringly tried, and I only listened, because I couldn't see her tiny chalkboard etchings very well. I was basically and begrudgingly disinterested but still managed to pull a low A average after a few exams. But then things started to heat up. New concepts were introduced and a new way of thinking about numbers was dumped on us "locked up" prisoners for the whole period while in that dreary classroom, every damn day. Mrs. H. kept right on smiling while exposing us to cockamamie instructions that sought to simplify mathematics and give us a strong foundation for future reckoning. She often said, "This way of figuring will help all of you succeed in algebra, in ninth grade." Really? Well, she figured wrongly as I began to struggle. The torpid topic of "Base 10," as an easy way to calculate equations, seemed to buffalo me. It was supposedly a logical method to break down sets of numbers while adding, subtracting, multiplying and dividing, and at the same time properly wiring the adolescent brain for more difficult problems yet to come. However, it wasn't logical to me. I just didn't get it; it didn't make any sense. I could come up with the correct answer every time but not with the convoluted and asinine way that Mrs. H. wanted us to. All homework handed in was graded. I kept receiving incompletes because while my answers were correct, my derivations of them were "kooky

and incorrect," lamented Mrs. H. At one point, the teacher
even accused me of parental help because of my correct
conclusions but faulty reasoning. My ensuing low test
grades reflected my blatant disregard of the principles she
was teaching even though all my answers were spot on. My
professor pop was outraged and blew up, as expected. His
kind of civil engineering math started with algebra and he
saw no value in this baseless *garbage* that passed as
mathematics. I was exasperated, frustrated and failing.
What could I do? Maybe start wearing my specs so I could
actually see her detailed explanations on the black
chalkboard? Maybe have an upperclassman tutor me?
Maybe have my already agitated and impatient father start
assisting me with my homework? Holy shit, no; *No* to
those last two suggestions. Also, I had mistakenly thought
that joining the teacher's math club would bolster my
GPA, or at least give me some needed brownie points, but
I was mistaken. It was a waste of after-school time, and I
quit after a few tired sessions. So, I became four-eyes again,
started reading the math textbook religiously, and slowly
began to play the game, the way the teacher wanted. My
grades shot up, my ego was still bruised, but I got my
nagging old man off my back. Years later while taking
algebra, and finally REALLY comprehending math for the
first time in my young life, it dawned on me that now I

understood what Mrs. H. was cackling about in seventh-grade arithmetic class. Base 10 numerology was obvious, now. Not then, but now. Too little, too late. Maybe I should have jumped ahead directly into ninth-grade algebra after sixth grade? But after I faltered and stumbled in the sixth-grade numbers game toward the end of that year, I ended up sucking wind while stuck in both non advanced seventh and eighth grade mathematics classes and, frankly, did not learn much. Oh, and that upcoming eighth-grade math class was *taught* by yet another ineffectual blithering blatherer; we'll get to that debacle later.

11

Math Club

My father knew nothing about it and my mom did not rat me out as she pushed me to join the junior high math club, run by Mrs. H., the confused and disorganized seventh-grade math teacher. But maybe I was the confused and disorganized idiot? Sometimes it was hard to tell, especially the way the year was unfolding thus far. Anyhow, my mother thought it would be prudent on my part to ingratiate myself on a teacher I loathed, to help boost my class average. It seemed like a blatantly bold scheme because as you readers have probably already figured out I despised mathematics of all kind, and still do! However, I thought that the after-school club, that met weekly, would be a series of mini tutoring lessons that would greatly help my numerically challenged brain to get caught up, so to speak. That was my assumption. Wrong. It was a lame and tame classroom full of whimsy and bullshit as the teacher sought to play "math" games and puzzles instead of teaching me what I didn't "get" in her daily class. The students present, none of whom were my friends, were enthusiastic and eager to suck up to her and participate in mindless mathematical drivel. I just sat there like a stone, and stone-faced as well. And it was obvious that those certain pupils were in line way ahead of me for brown nose-of-the-year honors. I just couldn't compete with them and, didn't want to. After a few such sessions, I quit. Mom was disappointed, I was chagrined and depressed. It had been a valiant effort on my part, but the math club was not a fun place to be. MATH was definitely NOT fun for me! Although, to this day, I still correct my longtime tax accountant whenever certain *numbers* don't add up in my favor, if you know what I mean. And I did get an A in calculus in college, by the way. Go figure. Perhaps seventh-grade arithmetic was an aberration that caught my cerebral cortex off guard? Or maybe I was just an arrogant and inconsolable dumbbell that harbored anger and animosity toward my own failure to secure a coveted spot in the high math class (eighth-grade pre-algebra) that all my buddies were in? Hopefully it was the former, but most likely the latter.

12

The Flintlock Free Library

Good ole' Mr. Flintlock, who upon his passing, willed a large portion of his estate to run our town's costless public library in perpetuity. Henry Flintlock was locally born and became a bank teller, a wealthy banker in Minnesota, and eventually secretary of the U.S. Treasury. In the mid-19th century, he and his family members established the stately and conveniently located library building on Elm Street, without a penny's donation from the curious and mostly illiterate villagers. Thusly, even as a tiny tyke, it had been a pleasure for me to walk there in the 20th century to freely check out *Curious George* books and other age appropriate reading material. Obviously, adult books were present too, as well as ancient artifacts, local historical memorabilia, and an authentic, large, black, bearskin rug on the floor near the entrance, complete with the real stuffed head and snarling teeth! Though we junior high students had access to the large, study-carrell-lined high school library, sometimes a book or quiet time was needed on a Saturday, when the school library was shuttered. I was a regular customer and a card-carrying Flintlock Free Library member since kindergarten and had gone home with armloads of publications for years. Lots of my school buds also partook of that solemn but well stocked book repository. It was a hallowed, nostalgic place to visit, even at that time. There was a locked, book return drop box, hidden by trimmed hemlocks, next to the front door, for Sunday and evening book deposits when the library was closed. One day, on a whim, as my mom was carefully inserting a few overdue volumes through the box slot on top, I mischievously started fiddling around with the lock at the box's base. It was a large, brass padlock with four, numbered tumblers on its bottom end. With my younger sister looking on, I dialed in four consecutive zeros and the lock popped open. I opened the box door, caught the books mom was feeding it and handed them back to her as my sister started cracking up. Mom was surprised but not amused. "How did you open it?" she exclaimed, as I hurriedly closed and locked things back up again. "Lucky guess," I answered, rather boastfully. However, now I had a secret that only my sister and I knew. But it didn't last. The numbers had been changed by our next visit and, try as I might, I could not break the code. My sister laughed again, this time at my ineptitude as a bragging wannabe safe cracker. My mother was happy that I was stymied. "There will be no burglars or thieves in our family," she admonished me. Maybe a future dentist, but not a thief. Wait a minute, aren't they one and the same?

13

The New Feminist Agenda?

Oh goody, finally a class I knew I would excel at: English. NOT! Although a fast reader and decent composer of the written word in elementary school, seventh grade English with that brand spanking new teacher would prove provocative, exasperating and troubling. I was all ready; unfortunately, Miss S. incorporated basic English tenets with biased personal tirades that she willfully foisted on the majority redneck offspring in her classes. Well, I wasn't one of THEM, but still…. I lived and breathed among them, befriended them and most assuredly had them rub off on me. We were basically a small farming town, with a junior college up on the hill, a county jail, a sheriff, a police chief, and one traffic light. The common villagers were mostly conservative in nature, bigoted, opinionated, suspicious, and with a homespun twangy wisdom that was both aggravating and charming. We filed into English class that first morning, took seats and saw a long dark-haired, slightly chubby, scowling young women at the front of the room who blandly introduced herself as Miss S., the new seventh-grade English teacher. Most of us nodded in return. She innocently asked us if we had read any good books over the previous summer vacation. A few pupils blurted out some inane works, but most of us sat still, ready for directions, not questions. And that's when her gloves came off. She turned angry with the paltry answers and stood there with her face getting redder and redder, as my eyes grew wider and wider. Then, within a few minutes, she proceeded to berate us for not reading anything worthwhile, for not being up to date on current events, for not embracing liberal philosophy, and for not stepping up for women's rights. What? She was mad for some reason and laid into us for our seeming lack of left-leaning ideology. How did she know? This was her first job, her first day ON the job. Was this how the rest of the year would go? Holy hell! She quickly dismissed the males in the class as chauvinistic, misogynistic fools (what did those big words even mean to an eleven-year-old boy?) and proceeded to glare and scoff at the squirming girls. Then she bodaciously blurted out the names Betty Friedan, Gloria Steinem, Shirley Chisholm, and Angela Davis. She looked around for a positive female response but our fellow "sisters" sat motionless and unresponsive. And then the coup de grace: she nonchalantly pontificated, "I burned my bra this morning, did any of you, girls?" What? Most of the farmers' daughters wore plaid, long sleeve shirts and OshKosh denim overalls, with maybe a training bra thrown in for good measure. And the rest of the non farming females were similar in appearance and also had not been "clothing radicalized" by the *left*, so to speak. As the girls blushed, Miss S. continued to rant and rave about their small-minded, provincial attitudes. We boys were a nonentity to her, thus far. So, we just sat there, in a confused and stuporous state. Sure, the townspeople read the local papers and watched Walter Cronkite religiously on the boob tube but in the fall of 1971 conservatism was the prevailing attitude in our sleepy village. How dare she come here and spill her vulgar, antimale, feminist agenda on helpless *oxymoronic* morons in junior high? At least, that's what I thought at the time. Many of us had heard of Woodstock, free love, sexual experimentation, and the ensuing second wave of the feminist movement but I didn't think it would rudely slap me upside the head in seventh-grade English class. Some of us were still reading childish rubbish and Superman comic books with a smattering of *National Geographic* and *Reader's Digest* stories, here and there. We weren't politically savvy beyond what political candidates our parents voted for. But there she stood, lecturing us as adults. She took our innocence away in a hurry but at least made us think about things other than our own homely and pedestrian lives. We took it in the gut that first day, but were forced to return to that witch's den over and over again. I wonder if any girls told their parental units about the "new" teacher. I never mentioned her antics to my folks. Nevertheless, every English class for the rest of the year was adulterated with her brand of feminine activism and loathing of the male sex. I guess I did learn some readin' and writin' from her but suffered with B-level grades in that course. I will tell you that she was gone by the time I reached high school. She had secretly dated and married a professor from the local college, quietly quit her teaching career and disappeared from town. Go figure. Was she in fact a formerly jilted lover, a phony progressive, a faux feminist demagogue, bipolar, a frustrated bitch, and a mediocre teacher? Perhaps some of the above? Instead of following the infamous quote that famed Australian feminist Irina Dunn once wrote, "A woman needs a man like a fish needs a bicycle," Miss S. seemed to have capitulated to a different agenda. "She snagged a sucker and skedaddled out of Dodge," the home crowd would later knowingly remark. And I often wondered if any of the former underage *home gurls* had ever burned any of their undergarments? Maybe, instead of washing them?

14

Shag

E.S. was a man's man. He was rough, tough, and made the Marlboro Man appear wimpy. He was a middle-aged, powerfully built, former gym teacher who reputedly smoked like a chimney and drank like a fish. He was Rambo and Jaws, rolled into one being. A real-life action hero with a crew cut, a nasty disposition, but an appropriate counterbalance to the "messed up" counterculture of the '60s and '70s: our principal! He even had a derogatory sounding nickname – *Shag*, sort of a shortened version of his last name. However, no matter his loud mouthed and uncouth reputation, I believe he was needed for those times. And not just for the high school, but as principal for junior high, as well. Grades 7-12 were under his command and control, starting with morning announcements, which he blared out with that gravelly, baritone voice of his. As a newly minted seventh grader, my interaction with him was minimal. Sure, I saw him storm down the hallways at times, or hear him lecture a student for poor deportment, or witness him hiding a lit cigarette behind his back while chatting up a pretty female teacher next to his first floor office, off the lobby. But that was about it. I was never sent to the principal's office like some of the school's obvious miscreants. I heard rumors that they were often "bullied" into straightening up, or else. However, the school board must have approved of his administration and ministrations for he was a longtime fixture at our fine institution. I had no complaints, I steered clear of that oversized pit bull and only greeted him if absolutely necessary, whenever I physically encountered him, which was not often. *Shag*: the man, the legend?

15

The Wall

Oh, the infamous "wall." A place of peace, love, amateur psychoanalysis, smokes, and pot. A place of lunchtime reverie and escape. A place to ponder, denounce, unwind and get stoned. It was a nondescript stone wall, not 100 feet from the windowless side of our brick "penitentiary," bordering a parking lot. However, it had a steep, grassy, slope on the side facing away from our school, where *indulging* students could hide unseen from the authorities. Even we dorky seventh graders had heard about it. It was where all the supposedly "cool" kids went for unstructured lunch period, after a bout with close by Maxie's gas station, which was conveniently located near the base of the hill. Maxie's was where all the sweets and cigarettes were usually purchased. I easily could have gone to that neatly arranged slate fence also, but never did. It was basically reserved for the presumed *bad element* in school, where "those" students of all ages would gather as if for a daily, hippie-inspired, *party*. It was often mentioned in hushed tones as if a holy shrine and place of worship; and to not let any nosy teacher within earshot know it was being talked about. "A den of inequity," as allegedly hard-drinking, chain-smoking and positive role model Principal *Shag* would frequently yell out whenever he angrily raided that wall unannounced – at least a few times a month but not during the winter months, when student tracks packed down the snow into a muddy, cigarette butt filled area. Now, I had gone by it hundreds of times, in the summer months, on the way to the village pool across the street from it. It was nothing really, just flat gray stones arranged as a barrier in 1939, when our present high school was built. However, it had become a symbol of rebellion during the turbulent '60s and '70s, much to the consternation of the staff at our "house of detention." I remember sitting on it as a senior student, just for laughs, and just for a moment's photograph. I didn't want to get caught being anywhere near it. However, as I was leaving it that day, I thought of all the fervent, deep and anguished conversations that must have taken place there over the years, and all the illicit drugs that had been shared and consumed there, as well. But there was no evidence of graffiti or lasting stains to speak of. If only it had eyes, ears and a mouth. I would have loved to have heard its stories. It is not a metaphor, it still physically exists, but it is only a stone wall, or should I say, *stoned* wall.

16

Early Laugh Tracks

As I have undoubtedly mentioned a few times in this volume and in a few previously published ones, although my nuclear family members had senses of humor, our collective, *old world*, conservative, philosophy was to remain stuck in a stoic state of mind most of the time. No highs and no lows. That meant that excessive demonstrations of unbridled and spontaneous levity were strongly frowned upon. And we weren't even Amish! Appearing serious meant that you were indeed a serious person and not a fool. And there I was, a comedian just bursting to get out, stymied by my own kin! Now don't get me wrong, we did watch television shows and sitcoms, before there was cable, sometimes howling with mirth at the goings on of the comics on the small screen. However, that was considered sanctioned and rationed humor, to be indulged in for a very brief time and then turned off, literally. So, to circumvent the prevailing "Somber Town" attitude in my household and to get my fill of lunacy, I had to quietly and surreptitiously sneak around on Saturdays and Sundays, not only to watch Looney Tunes cartoons but my favorites such as *The Three Stooges* and the

Hanna-Barbera clan of goofballs and wise guys. I always got caught but strangely was not punished or even admonished. Nothing. Just some eye rolls from Grandpa Pete, who gave up on me as a bona fide grandson years ago, and some disappointing shrugs from my old man. We only had one black-and-white tele; that's why I was always nabbed, sometimes while chuckling at Woody Woodpecker's crazy antics or roaring at Bullwinkle's sarcastic stupidity. It's worth noting that Sesame Street, Mr. Roger's Neighborhood and H.R. PufnStuf were never on my palate of shows to see. I was a hardcore wisenheimer, even back then, and not a whimsical, Mickey Mouse kind of jokester. Then, slowly, my comedic habit spread to the evenings as well. *Laugh-In*, *Hee Haw*, *Sanford and Son*, plus the endless variety of programs featuring the big stars of yesteryear like Bob Hope, Phyllis Diller, Lucille Ball, Rodney Dangerfield, Jackie Gleason, etc., also kept me entertained. And don't forget the Marx Brothers, whose lengthy films were infrequently aired, but were welcome treats for true aficionados of their unique brand of "funny business." Sure, I watched the CBS news every evening at 6:30 as a serious ritual with the male elders in my home but secretly had the upcoming schedule of comedic shows memorized as well. And on most Sundays a certain presentation became the special laugh track amusement of the week. Believers in good, wholesome "fun," even my stodgy folks would take a midday break to view constantly rerun Abbott and Costello movies, starting at 11:30 a.m. and ending at 1 o'clock. Grandpa would often poke his nose out of his downstairs bedroom and watch some of the shenanigans of Bud and Lou as they stumbled and bumbled hilariously on screen. Promptly at 1 p.m., after finishing up our snacks, we would click off the tube, sadly disband and go do our own things. I sorely missed some of the recently cancelled shows such as *Get Smart*, *The Monkees* and *The Munsters*, but had many other offbeat series to look forward to. It seemed as though my *jesterous* personality only grew, thanks to the fodder provided me through television and junior high school monkeyshines. I guess my parents had put up with me as best as they could, for I was basically a "handicapped" child in their sorrowful eyes. I was good in athletics and an above average student, but I HAD to be "disabled," right? How could any kid of theirs love insects, amphibians and comedy so much? It wasn't natural, it wasn't normal, but it was for me.

17

Sighting the Sako

This was serious business all right. My grandpa Pete, father and I were going afield to one of the many grassy haunts around town, to practice shooting and to sight our Sako (a top Finnish hunting rifle company renowned for its accuracy and durability) long guns for the upcoming deer hunting season which was still months away. Must-do and perpetual family projects were put on hold on those select autumn weekends for us menfolk to become transformed into "country gentlemen" and go gunning in the woods for "fun." Good thing I enjoyed it because any other seventh grader with an inkling of softheartedness or ounce of wimpiness would have felt abhorrence at the idea of practicing killing small animals for sport and recreation, just to kill even larger animals for sport, recreation and food! And there I was, a so called animal lover and amateur naturalist, gamely dressed up in camo attire and willingly following the two adult male lions in my family pride to go small game hunting. WTF? However, it was a necessary ritual in our rural village. Most of the farming community hunted and sharpened up their sharpshooting skills on a regular basis. That was normal in those times and in our

NEW neck of the woods, so to speak. But how did OUR family get involved? My immigrant but city bred pop was a white collar college professor, not some roughneck, drunken hunter that reveled in killing harmless animals. What had happened to turn a smart city kid into a good ole boy? And how did a tennis and piano playing, smart aleck and anxious junior high student get coerced to play along and start packing heat for the hunt? I was no vegan, but still…. And my workaholic and grumpy grandpa Pete was an old salt, Estonian immigrant farmer from the old country; hunting, shooting, gutting, skinning, etc. was old hat to him. Of course you had to practice to make perfect. It made sense. But wait a minute! How did all this come to pass? I believe it was succumbing to *bad* influences all around us. C.R., a somewhat irascible neighbor and fuel oil owner/delivery man, always bantered local hogwash with my old man whenever he drove his tanker truck over to fill up our house tanks with fuel oil. Between chomping on his unlit stub of a cigar, he would regale my father with his hunting and shooting exploits, most of which were true. My mom would have to physically extricate my wide-eyed father from the rich storytelling of the homebred hombre from next door. He was the same long-winded local bloke whose son used to be my BFF in the very early grades of grammar school. Slowly, he convinced my pop that he would never fit into the local "scene" unless he changed his ways. Grizzled and rotund C.R. quite rudely but laughingly told my father that he was looked upon by the male village "elders" as a perpetual outsider and a "liberal" professor; at least that was the word on the street. So, my father converted overnight it seemed. He proceeded to transmute almost daily from a most intellectual professor by sunlight into an all-around redneck on selected nights, minus the drinking and skirt chasing. Why he chose that road remains a mystery. Maybe he needed to get away from his own work-obsessed father who was living with us? Perhaps he was "bored" of teaching and coming home nightly to a "boring" existence filled with "boring" projects to do and a "boring" family to boot? But HE was the one that insisted on running a *conservative* household with well done steaks and no coffee. We thought we were only obliging him. Who knows, but his abrupt change influenced me greatly as we shall see. A distant neighbor, up the steep, dead-end street from our newly built domicile, was an avid raccoon hunter; we could clearly hear his outdoor caged coon dogs baying nightly just before he went hunting with them. Of course, neighborly C.R. invited pop to go along for a routine "joyous" hunt with him and that "raccoon hunting neighbor" up the street. Pop didn't even have to bring anything, no gun, no license, no nothing; just himself. Well, I guess he loved the adventure because he was soon applying for a coveted full-carry pistol permit and was caught grinning while thumbing through gun magazines on a nightly basis. Oh, and C.R. *secretly* signed him up for the local but statewide top ranked village pistol team. What? My dad was not a hunter, a shooter, or a ragamuffin local with a penchant for chewing tobacco and trouble making. But he showed up at the gun club on time on a fateful Wednesday evening practice session, was handed a specially weighted 22 caliber American Standard automatic pistol and was quickly taught how to fire at a hanging paper, bullseyed target. And he made the team on his first foray into target shooting. He was a natural, so he told my mom. C.R. had correctly guessed that my father had hidden *homeboy* tendencies and was a natural fit with the raucous and formerly suspicious natives that now had new respect for this accent laden newcomer. As a gifted all-around athlete, of course the old man had talent for whatever sport or skill he tried. I wasn't surprised. Thus began an odyssey into the world of target shooting and hunting for my dad and me. And, after the shooters at the club found out that pop was a gifted amateur horologist, they inundated him with all sorts of watches and jewelry to repair for them. He was actually much better than the jeweler in town, who also started sending him "tough" cases to repair. Pop only charged for parts because it was a hobby for him. Maybe that's why he always had "something" in his advanced home office set-up to fix. Then someone from his club gave him a jammed and gummed up gun to look at. After he expertly fixed it, he became an indispensable part of the shooting gang that practiced on Wednesdays and shot competitively on Fridays, all winter long. He frequently made the top four spots for counting up final scores when he competed on those Friday evening jousts. And it didn't take dad long to procure equipment to make bullets at home, as a fun exercise and to save a buck or two. He bought powder packets, primers and brass casings. We cast the lead bullets ourselves with a mini casting crucible resembling a Fry Daddy after scouring parking lots for lead balancing weights that fell off of car tires. After the slugs were made, specialized equipment was used to put together the actual bullet, complete with carefully weighed gunpowder, a seated primer, and by using a crimping machine at the end. He had become a real firearms connoisseur and a self-made gunsmith. Of course he did. What couldn't that man do? Meanwhile, I heard scuttlebutt from my mom that his fellow highbrow professors were puzzled and getting worried about his association with local "hoodlums" and unsavory types that actually "shot" weapons at defenseless animals. It was bad enough that he now possessed a permit to legally purchase and carry weapons, but the deer hunting? The coon hunting? The grouse and pheasant hunting? Luckily, he found a few like-minded souls in the college community and they decided to keep things quiet so as not to overly alarm their mostly elitist and left-leaning campus brethren. I was a party to all of this and grew up with firearms in the household. It was no big deal to see multiple guns, shells and magazines lying around in his private office. Nothing was ever locked up. Guns were everywhere in our town and there was virtually no crime. Hmm…. Anyhow, I never took over his horological or gunsmithing hobbies, but I did have an affinity for shooting. We went to the club's indoor gun range many times to practice. I was actually rather good for a beginner. But that's where it ended for me. Although a decent shot, I never went deer or coon hunting. It just wasn't in me. Even Grandpa Pete only went out twice. However, I DID go out with pop and my grandpa to sight our deer rifles on targets and rascally woodchucks. Those subterranean rodents didn't know what hit them while we were stealthily waiting for them to surface, often more than fifty yards away. That's how pop got ready for deer hunting season. And that's why I suddenly and eerily felt comfortable in seventh-grade math class while sitting next to E.W., that November of 1971. I enthusiastically and somewhat sarcastically complimented him on his red and black hunting jacket with a prominently pinned deer hunting license on its back. But he was sincerely damn proud of it and told me he could hardly wait to get home and go hunting on his farm on the first day of the season. Twelve-year-olds were allowed to get a big game buck permit back then and many boys wore appropriate hunting attire to class throughout the short season as badges of courage and manhood. And as I intuitively observed, the female students with no big career ambitions probably and hopelessly saw the writing on the wall early. They would most likely marry or cohabitate with those *boyz* in the near future, the same ones they were currently rolling their eyes at, much like their mothers did with their fathers. It was the inevitable circle of familiarity and breeding that happened in small towns. The hunting, killing and eating of butchered vittles was considered normal for our pint-sized village, and my immediate family, composed of former city slickers, now proudly partook of it. E.W. and I were not friends, but we exchanged a few pleasant syllables as his fellow cohorts nodded and voiced their approval of me and my intimate know-how about shootin,' huntin,' and making my own ammunition. It was nice to be accepted by both my fellow snooty and intelligent college professors' offspring and by the vast majority of *country cousins* with guns on their minds and in their hands. I eventually became a dentist. I heard that E.W. became an animal husbandry professional, namely an artificial inseminator of female cows! Both of us treated unwilling and nervous patients. I guess we both ended up more alike than not. How ironic is that?

18

More Shootin'

Our family field trips started while I was in elementary school. They were nothing special, just sporadic fall weekend fare consisting of a middle-aged married couple and their two young kids out for a crime-free and people-free walk through fields and streams. Back then, even our local ticks didn't have Lyme causing bacteria in them. It was a giant and safe neighborhood to live in. Our very rural and hilly farming region had lots of unposted, state-owned meadows and glens to hike in throughout the 1960s and '70s and it didn't cost my frugal father a dime. Now, while appearing to be sickeningly sweet family outings filled with love and goodwill, pop usually had ulterior motives while in the woods and valleys, regardless of we three following him as determined intrepid interlopers. I mean, he acknowledged us; he gave us breaks and even let us sip some water from his canteen as needed. But every autumn he was there on his messianic missions, looking for deer trails for the upcoming hunting season and for practice, using his Sako 30-06 hunting rifle and Smith and Wesson 357 Magnum, scoped, handgun. He would set up targets and fire away, with us covering up our ears and patiently waiting for the shooting to be over. Of course, I got my chance to handle his favorite pistol and always remarked at the jolting kickback it had. I swear my father turned into a *redneck rebel* on those jaunts in wooded grasslands. Mom and sis never said a word as they trundled behind him as he nosed around trees and ancient stone walls, looking and memorizing the terrain. Besides firing off a few rounds myself, I was busy indulging my zoological passions, observing the miniature fauna on those excursions, namely, looking for and catching insects and any creepy crawly thing that crossed my path. I flipped over logs, rocks and scattered the newly fallen leaves to find salamanders, toads, grasshoppers, mantids, etc. Pop saw me doing my naturalistic "thing" and never said a word. At least his son was manly enough to expertly handle a heavy rifle and six-shooter, and could knock off aluminum cans with ease, even while aiming and squeezing the trigger one handed! I liked the smell of gun powder smoke as I shot the very bullets I had made with my father during the winters. My open-minded mom was tolerant of the shooting, but my younger sister never got the chance to fire any family weapons. They were the support team only. And once pop was satisfied with his target practice and deer sleuthing results, he lightened up and usually enjoyed the remainder of the day. We followed suit. The hikes were interesting fun, with my old man planning to strike down Bambi; me, looking and finding my fill of weird and esoteric arthropods, and my mom and sister tagging along for the sunshine and exercise. Nevertheless, I also remember many mild and tame picnic-type walkabouts, sans visible shootin' irons, when we as a family went wild blueberry picking in the deep woods behind the college or just took a quick trek behind our house for no reason except to get out into the open and explore nature. Sometimes pop took his expensive Leica camera along. He frequently surprised me at his multifaceted approach to life and relaxation, but he always packed some hidden heat, just in case, even on those tame expeditions. A rightful city boy had turned into a country clodhopper, at least on those select weekends, even though his day job was as a suit-and-tie-clothed, learned, college professor. Such was his quixotic and eccentric adulthood behavior, as far as a twelve-year-old could ascertain. I relished the fact that he and I spent some quality time together, albeit with him scouting and shooting and me digging and collecting. I forgot about my miserable math shortcomings and school bullshit for a while and that made those trips all the more worthwhile. And I believe those relatively banal times influenced me at some basal, subconscious level, as well. I have my own firearms now and can still shoot straight, and

love to get out into nature at every chance. However, the
deer and the antelope can play in peace. I don't hunt.

19

Girls

Girls, Girls, Girls, a major pop rock hit in 1987 by the metal "hair band" Mötley Crüe, aptly sums up my juvenile anticipatory attitude toward the fair sex upon starting seventh grade in 1971. Nothing lascivious, mind you, but more than mere curiosity. Thanks to testosterone, my gray matter and body were rapidly changing; new feelings of desire were stirring, mentally and physically. Okay, I was an adolescent horny toad but couldn't do anything about it; not yet, anyway. I was twelve, was relatively hairless, and longed for some type of lady companionship, no matter how primitive. I knew what girls looked like under their undies; I had a slew of National Geographic journals, with naked foreign women portrayed in them, which I perused on a regular basis. I also possessed a few anatomy volumes that I had purchased with my own allowance. What I lacked was an older brother with stacks of *Playboy* or *Penthouse* magazines under his bed to gawk at. But I managed to glimpse the unclothed female form on a regular basis, just not in person. Now, some of the girls in my grade hit puberty early and instantly became objects of my affection, albeit from a distance. That's how heterosexual manhood began for me, in lurches and spurts. Nevertheless, in spite of my newfound masculine *swagger* and unwholesome thoughts, I did not hook up with a single female in seventh grade, or eighth for that matter. I was way too shy to approach good looking gals or to even mention my lustful thoughts to anyone of the opposite sex. The older females were off-limits for us insignificant posers, and the certain libidinous ones, "that were willing and able," seemed to instinctively know a sexual coward when they saw one. Plus, having relatively dark skin and an ethnic sounding surname did not instill manly confidence in me, either. Sure, I had many girl FRIENDS that liked me, but as inappropriate as it sounds, I wanted a bit more, even at that young age. Anyhow, my inner nerd won out and I sadly remained celibate throughout my junior high tenure, but not by choice.

20

No Hoops for You!

All right, I admit it, I basically sucked at basketball. Although good at ping pong and tennis, handling the round ball with relatively small hands was not my forte. Oh, sure, I could dribble, pass and had a rather good shot, if left unguarded, that is. And I easily passed all the fundamental basketball requirements in Phys Ed as demanded by the teacher, Mr. K. And I slightly excelled when playing the mandatory "shirts and skins" games during the gender separated gym classes. You know, half the boys were shirtless, and half kept their shirts on so players could readily differentiate between fellow teammates and opponents. A friend of mine, B.H., seemed to like the shirtless concept and sometimes flaunted his lack of attire around school, much to his ensuing discipline invoking detriment. Anyway, I wasn't a klutz and could make a running layup and felt comfortable at the foul line. I even swished a few foul shots now and then. I instinctively realized that Mr. K., my biased nemesis and JV basketball coach, was actively looking for future stars, not only for his team but for the varsity, as well. We were the minor leaguers and he was the scout, scouring the field to pick out that year's rising rim-jocks. It was his job. My job was to perform as well as possible and maybe try out for the junior high basketball team. I admit it was an infantile fantasy of mine back then. The glory, the camaraderie, the anticipated acceptance from the local male hatchlings, the girls…. Well, maybe not the girls. But, anyway, I thought I had gathered enough skills to confidently try out for the team. I was athletically inclined and fleet-footed, but I didn't have a backboard and basket at home to practice on like most of my fellow competitors did. It was a few weeks of after-school, daily workouts in the gym under the watchful gaze of Mr. K., who yelled out directions, blew his loud whistle endlessly, and silently judged we putrid players as we tried to execute a proper jump shot, a pick and roll play, and just plain dribble the length of the court without losing the ball. Of course, we newbies knew that most of the *veteran* eighth grade players and the tallest kids would make the club. But there was a plethora of us smaller and quick fellows, jockeying for a few coveted spots on that "prestigious" roster. Nonetheless, some would-be ballers had to be cut, and I was one of them. I had tried my hardest but had no older basketball playing brother that could vouch for me. I was an athletic nobody. My "effeminate" racquet sports gave me no credibility whatsoever and perhaps elicited ridicule and contempt for me instead. Mr. K., the *homeboy* former high school star athlete turned gym teacher/coach, probably did the fledgling team a favor by casting me aside, because some of the other guys were in fact much better than I and deserved to play. But not all. And that's what really hurt. There were a few cagers that I could best in every category, yet they made the squad and I did not. Was it just bad luck? Was it the usual bigoted bullshit from a coach who definitely was not a fan of mine? Was it a last second and mindless decision that just wasn't that important in the long run? This was junior high, you know, not the NBA, for God's sake. However, I was bitterly disappointed, and it took a while for me to shake it off. It would have been nice to belong to a group of sportsmen, on a team that already had fan support, and become prepared to someday play varsity ball. Well, it never happened. My hoop dream popped, and I went back to hitting little, white, fuzzy, balls again. Not to mention even smaller, hard, plastic ping pong balls. But the remembrances of those tryouts of yesteryear are still with me. I would have been happy just to ride the bench as a seventh grader; perhaps I had been the last man cut? Ah, memories. By the way, whenever my former track-and-swimming superstar son is home, we play a little one-on-one basketball at the local YMCA gym, using our own ball, of course. We wear our favorite team's jerseys; we hustle, hit jumpers, block shots, rebound, drive to the basket and probably look good from a distance. But whenever we get asked to join a group of guys already playing, we respectfully decline because although athletically blessed, we BOTH basically suck at basketball.

21

Padding a Future Résumé?

What is it with boys and badges, and uniforms, and conformity, while at the same time being encouraged to follow the American dream of individuality and personal freedoms? Let me try to explain. Seventh grade not only opened up our formerly closeted world to deal with more students, a philosophically diverse faculty and hot button topical issues of the day, but also a plethora of clubs and organizations to possibly join. Golly, sometimes I felt like going back to elementary school, with only 25 other students, one classroom, one teacher, and one bathroom. Ah, but choices make the world go 'round. Or, do they? Although boldly seeking to strike out as unique individuals and to not "follow the crowd," the various clubs and service organizations at our school seemed to discourage that attitude and offered a twisted sense of safety zones and tribalism for like-minded pupils. I also lump high school athletics into that lot. I realize that it was important to be exposed to disparate ideas, virtuous missions and sports, but at the same time did certain students cloister together as immunity against others? The farm boys bonded, the obvious jocks stuck together, the musicians and artist-types had their own cliques; so why have officially sanctioned *activities* as well? To further put wedges into the fragile psyches of students? I don't know and I'm no psychologist, or even a psychiatrist. Anyhow, what made a few of my male classmates choose to be safety patrol guards, complete with white harnesses and badges? You know, the annoying assholes that lorded over us *schleppers* as we were trying to cross the streets around the school grounds in the mornings and at dismissal; the same jerks that admonished and ridiculed us if we failed to use a designated crosswalk. You know, those guys that most of us hated. Kind of like the similar and goofy AV nerds that THOUGHT they were cool. There were no girl guards, just junior high boy guards. However, did those predisposed boys enjoy bossing people around? Was it out of a sense of arrogance and justified bullying? Did they aspire to be in law enforcement some day? I don't know and don't care. But there was also the girl's only sewing club, run by the gorgeous home economics teacher, the Future Farmers of America club, the varsity club, the morning announcement club, etc. Some, like sex-separated scouting and coed 4-H, were administration approved afterschool entities, but nonetheless became part of the educational morass anyway. And some, like scouting, had uniforms and codes of conduct to follow, as well. But did lazily signing up for a

host of organizations earn a bootlicking student Brownie
points or help pad a future résumé? Maybe so. Sometimes,
parental pressures and having an older sibling already
involved made it mandatory to join up. Sort of like being
born into a particular religion; sometimes you had no
choice of hypocritical dogma. But what about having a
paper route? Did that count as well? I remember that a few
ballyhooed sons of local town officials dutifully rose at 5
a.m. each morning and jumped on their banana bikes, to
deliver paper rags to the townsfolk and make a few coins in
return. I had heard that many presidents of our country
did the same thing to learn responsibility and a sense of
pride through contrived deprivation and service. Was there
indeed a connection, or at least a correlation? Was having a
paper route listed on a résumé a ticket to success or was it a
joke? Besides a few bucks, what was the real ulterior
motive, I suspiciously asked myself? I once questioned my
cynical old man if I needed to do that to become president
someday. He sarcastically laughed long and hard at my
query. "I'd like to see how many of those dumb-ass *boyz*
become ANYTHING someday, let alone president. They
aren't automatically entitled like the politically connected,
dumb-ass Kennedys, you know," he would gleefully
chortle. Therefore, I picked and chose my sports and
afterschool affiliations carefully and not just to look good

on paper. I don't know if other students were so inclined, or had mercenary thoughts in their heads that more was better, especially for college applications down the road? Nevertheless, most of my closest friends and I ended up in most of the same few associations. But did we do ourselves any favors by sticking together in the first place and not expanding our individual horizons, or was it just junior high and no biggie to commit to likeminded groups? I'm talking about NOT being a wanton joiner! I value my freedom of choice and never willfully padded my curriculum vitae with superfluous junk. I also greatly value being a G.D.I. (God damn independent) and probably always will be. I prefer not to be left alone but to be let alone. As a consequence, I never receive any dues or donation letters from former college fraternities because I had never joined any. Thank goodness.

22

Squeaky Pals

This is most likely how my friendship with F. started. It wasn't in the classroom as we hadn't had any classes together in elementary school, and it wasn't at lunchtime or on the playground. It was through the violin. Yes, that four-stringed, curvy, wooden implement that could sound like a screeching cat or squeaking mouse if improperly fingered and poorly stroked by a horsehair bow. Yes, THAT musical instrument. But how, and why? Here goes: In sixth grade, students were given the opportunity to choose a musical instrument to play. The instruments themselves plus all the lessons, notes and accoutrements were on the school's nickel. The logic was that not only would the rising redneck stalwarts be exposed to culturally highfalutin Bach and Beethoven, but that some of them would continue and join the always needy orchestra or band in our musically lackluster school. So, that's how F. and I first met. He had no prior musical experience but possessed a keen ear and good manual dexterity. I, on the other hand, already had a local reputation as a budding "piano man" around town. I had also participated in NYSSMA competitions since fifth grade and only took up the violin as a lark. But whereas F. had talent with that stringed piece of varnished lumber, I basically sucked at playing it. Although a master at note reading and rhythm, somehow I could not parlay my piano expertise to that danged, lacquered "Stradivarius." I valiantly kept trying and almost quit on many occasions. However, hanging out with that funny kid F. made me stay with it. E.G., my other close comrade, from our third grade days, also picked up the fiddle. So now there were three stooges, or suckers, that would hopefully populate the string section in the school's meager orchestra. When seventh grade started, F. and I began *weakly* lessons together during specially allotted school times and were placed together as a twosome in the orchestral string section by the harried music director. We were officially designated as second violin, second stand. There was only one weaker duo than we two string strokers, and they sat directly behind us. E.G. was one of them. So, under the haphazard tutelage and misguidance of Mr. Daye, our frazzled teacher and conductor, E.G., F. and I started fooling around, "practicing," "playing," and "performing" in the mistuned and frequently misfiring assemblage called the high school orchestra. Unfortunately, E.G. ended his musical career rather abruptly although our friendship never wavered. On the other hand, F. and I continued our verbal and musical assaults on the unwilling ears and nerves of fellow players, parents and Mr. Daye, and finished up as first violin, second stand, as seniors. And throughout our junior high schooling, we continued to cement a long-tenured friendship that endured like a long-running TV sitcom, all the way through the first two years of pharmacy college together; laughing and pulling outrageous stunts on unsuspecting saps with comedic regularity. During our high school incarceration, we also unwittingly accumulated other like-minded buddies who eventually participated with us in school sanctioned skits, sketches and PG-rated debauchery. E.G., N.K., L.B., G.P., P.M. and J.Logg were early male/female co-conspirators of our fun-loving posse and never once vacillated in supporting us. Anyhow, that's the way our friendship began, through our mutual love of horseplay and the "deranged" violin. Our humorous forays were tolerated by most teachers and students, maybe because we both came from professors' families and possessed high GPAs. I'm sure that helped us tremendously and gave us clout when trying to weasel out of tight situations that others did not find levitous, especially the school administration. Nevertheless, the real buffoonery and Monty Pythonesque ribald humor wouldn't commence full force until ninth grade, with our fledgling troupe trying to entertain our fellow troops, usually on a daily basis. Meanwhile, commiserating and bonding with a like-minded seventh grader really livened me up, as well as those around us. And more audacious antics were yet to come.

23

Into the Closet

"Coming *out* of the closet" is a frequently bleated sentiment from today's disaffected and oppressed LGBTQXYZ community. However, back in '71, I was put *INTO* the closet, literally! As rookie junior high violinists, the janitor's tiny broom room across the hall from the music suite also doubled as our practice abode. It wasn't a punishment, though; that's where we novice, stringed instrument, impresarios were sent to hone our craft, while other students had their private lessons with Mr. Daye in the music chambers. Then we would switch places. Trundling off to that infamous berth, I would turn on the lone overhead light, close the heavy door, make some room among the dirty mops, brooms and pails, set up my notes on the unwieldly metal music stand, unpack my trusty school-issued fiddle, rosin up my bow and then furiously start scraping those darned strings. Good thing I was in a relatively soundproof enclosure, because the God-awful sounds emanating from that piece of wood wedged under my chin could have raised the dead! Perhaps that was the teacher's cunning plan after all: to let us practice but without noisily disturbing other students with our cacophony. Hmm…. Once in a while, a school custodian would politely knock and sheepishly poke his snout into "his" usurped space. I would annoyingly allow him to remove some tools of his trade, close the door and then kept at it. Hey, it was MY cubby hole for a half hour, dammit! Mr. Daye would punctually come around and exchange me for another student who would continue the wailing and hair-raising dissonance from that hobo hideaway. I would then get MY official lesson from the *Maestro*. And you all thought that only buckets and sweepers were stored in puny, dank, and stinky high school utility rooms. Not so, sometimes a "musician" would comically pop out of one, as if on cue.

24

The A.B. Affair

Well, it was more of an incident than an affair, but I liked the title, nonetheless. There I was, sequestered inside the custodial closet across from the music room, faithfully sawing away at my violin during a typical practice session when I heard some commotion outside in the hall. I cracked open the heavy door just enough to partially poke my head around it to see what all the brouhaha was about and wasn't disappointed. There was a teacher at each end of the hallway preventing students from entering it, and in the middle there appeared to be the aftermath of a fight. A.B., the big, loutish, school bully and resident troublemaker, who should have graduated years earlier, was on the floor, with his back slumped against the wall. Across from him stood another student, much smaller in size, and between them were two men who did not take kindly to misbehaving academicians, especially whenever A.B. was involved. The two grownups were none other than my hot-tempered gym teacher and the hot-tempered former gym teacher and no nonsense principal - *Shag*. Those were the wrong guys to mess with, on a good day. I did not see the episode go down but could still see the clenched fists of all the combatants involved. I quietly closed the door and kept on fiddling, like Nero did, while my high school "burned." Not really, though. Things quickly simmered down as if nothing had happened. I found out later that, as usual, A.B. had started a fight with another student and had to be physically restrained by those two faculty members. I also heard from reliable witnesses that the two adults each got a few good punches in. Everyone knew that it was a two on one handicap match but that asshole deserved it. A.B. most likely would have brashly won the day had it not been for him unluckily succumbing to the intervening *Shag* and Coach K., two men that probably relished working him over to deliver a powerful and positive message about deportment while on school property. A.B. disappeared shortly thereafter, and the school was finally rid of a menacing roughneck and hotdogger that should have been gone long ago. Fortunately, there were no deleterious repercussions to the school or students upon his exit. A.B. never returned with a pistol or bomb to assuage his damaged ego. We had gotten lucky. Conversely, today's *hip* culture of selfies, nihilistic narcissism and deranged self-esteem seems to be out of control, with seemingly *normal* students perpetrating violence on unsuspecting fellow pupils. We also had suicides, mental illnesses, depression, anxiety and broken homes in the '60s and '70s, yet somehow students kept it together without acting out on their frustrations. And we had almost unlimited access to legal and illegal firearms back in the day. Bullets and guns were sometimes lying around on kitchen tables, in broad daylight, and in *good* homes. However, there wasn't a single incident of murderous gunplay in our rustic village at the time. Our police chief and one lone officer had it easy; EVERYONE was armed and *dangerous* but no one pulled the trigger! I'm afraid times have really changed, and not for the better.

25

Wood Chipper

I had made it out of that quarterly course called Agriculture unscathed and had actually learned something. How useful it would be for me I didn't know. And the additional brain cells now taken up by images of Herefords, Guernseys and Jerseys were probably being wasted. Oh, well. At least I had a few extra brain cells to waste, I think. But now I had to steel myself for yet another quarter of similarly dubious but compulsory male education at our boondocks high school. Yes, daily, eighth period wood shop was in the docket and I had to take it, in the same bus garage building as Ag. had been before. The girls had two quarters of mandatory home economics with the beautiful Mrs. D.; we seventh-grade boys had elderly Mr. S., who proceeded to show us how to use the scary lathe, and how to properly whittle, sand, scrape, shape, buff, stain, lacquer, and polish a piece of damn kindling. All without using safety goggles, rip-proof gloves, smocks, ear plugs, signed non disclosure agreements, or even affidavits obviating the school for possible injuries sustained to students. It was the dark ages, before OSHA, HIPAA, PETA, ASPCA, etc. Well, maybe those acronyms were indeed around back then; however, our wood shop seemed immune to their dictums. Mr. S. started us off easy, though. He handed out heavy metal chisels, mounted blocks of timber for us peons onto individual wood-turning lathes, turned on the motors and told us to get cracking. What? I couldn't hear him well because of the instantaneous loud buzzing sound that surrounded us in that oversized classroom with a concrete floor. The wood was spinning at a dizzying speed in front of me, my heart was racing trying to keep pace with it, and I was sweating bullets. I wasn't prepared for this. Help! Then I stole some glances at a few farm boys near me. They seemed to know what they were doing. It made sense, though. Besides being braver than me, those *chiselers* approached ALL manual projects with gusto and zeal. Me, not really. But before long I got the knack (sorry about stealing that last line from the 1979, New Wave record album, *Get the Knack*, by The Knack, who else?), and while completely terrified out of my gourd, placed my delicate, future dentist hands near that rotating, whirling dervish and started "woodworking." I chiseled, I chipped, I sanded. Whew, I ended up covered with shavings and woody dander, down to my shoe tops. What a dusty and messy job it turned out to be, just to reduce a square into a circle. Anyhow, before long we started on our graded project. I made an undulated and ornate maple lamp stand, other kids made baseball bats and hammer handles. As long as it was circular in outcome, it was deemed successful. A-plus for me. Mr. S. drilled a hole in my piece for an electric cord to go through, after I had stained and polished it. It was fully functional and still stands in my boyhood home, complete with a lamp shade, receptacle and working light bulb. Of course, my old man had to wire it up first to make it work. Next up was hand scraping a stationary hunk of flat wood, after first carving it into a predesigned form using a stationary jigsaw. Careful with the fingers, those saws can really cut things off! I *jigged* and *jagged* a mahogany, Viking-inspired ship shape, hand carved a shallow square well in the middle of it, polished it, and voila: a wooden cheese serving plate complete with a dragon face on one end and a tail on the other. My mom still uses it. Another A for the non native, funny surnamed "foreigner," whose hands didn't shake and who could now handle and shape a hunk of lumber with ease. During that course I also made a few coarse cutting boards. My wife currently uses one. Oh, I forgot to tell you that one of my winter hobbies was plastic car model-making and gluing cut matchsticks together into complicated, miniature cricket cages and insect traps, complete with working latches and doors. So, I DID in fact possess a dollop of hand-eye coordination and felt comfortable while working with small, intricate objects. I guess dentistry was in my future, but who knew at the time? Anyhow, my initially trepidatious and short-lived, but straight A, "wooden" career was sadly over; time now for two highly anticipated quarters of music and art, respectively. Now, those two upcoming classes I knew I would excel at. But did I? Not so much, darn it, as we shall see.

26

Philco Schmilco

Okay, fasten your seatbelts; it was 1971 and time to buy our first color TV set. Out with the old and in with the new. Out with our old-fashioned, early '60s, wood cabinet-enveloped, black-and-white Philco, and in with…. Wait a minute, should we buy a Zenith or a Motorola product? Decisions, decisions. Even though from a conservative household, my father thought it was finally time to get with the program and invest in a color television. We did not binge watch but recreationally viewed a large number of disparate shows, nonetheless. The serious *CBS Evening News* and the gallivanting *Lawrence Welk Show* were two of them. Oh boy, now Walter Cronkite's various colored tie shades could be seen and we could finally learn if Arthur Duncan was really black, once and for all! And what about Saturday morning cartoons and Disney flicks? My sister and I could hardly wait to see Elmer Fudd and Pinocchio in living color. But which TV brand should the old man buy? Again, Zenith or Motorola? There were obviously other companies to choose from in our nearby cities but pop wanted to stay local, in case of a needed repair. And the only two locally available nameplates were, you guessed it, Zenith and Motorola. Both were popular, American made at the time (Motorola sold out to Japan in 1974 and Zenith eventually got bought out by South Korean LG Electronics), highly advertised, and ready to be delivered at a moment's notice. TVs were a burgeoning part of Americana, like cigarettes; everyone was encouraged to watch the boob tube and light up, sometimes at the same time. Some of the newer models even had a detachable ashtray built into the faux wood paneling on top of the bulky set. Gee whiz, pass me a Pall Mall, please, or a Virginia Slim, baby! Well, my father had come a long way to get the gumption to spend money and buy another piece of "required" 1970's family room entertainment, which would sit on our orange colored shag rug, next to the recently purchased hi-fi. Since he had already bought a top of the line Zenith turntable/radio/speakers combo from his pal P. at Fokay's Appliance Store, he figured a TV from him was next. Just down Main Street, Allen's Electronics sold Motorola, and though pop was also friends with the owner, he decided that he would give his business to P. instead. Now, dealing with P. was like something out of a bad movie. His all-purpose appliance store was in the former village butcher shop and was a busy center of business and arguments, alike. P. was a piece of work. Related to the same old immigrant (old immigrants came in the late 19th and early 20th centuries as opposed to recent immigrants like my folks, who came here after World War II) Russian clan that ran the grocery and liquor emporiums across the street and, married to a fourth grade teacher, he constantly feigned benevolence and restraint yet could easily be goaded into a nasty tempered frenzy if a sale went south. My dad loved to mess with him, just to provoke him and get his dandruff up. Although lifelong friends, pop always pushed his buttons and that made P. explode, but not before selling our family a product, such as a frig or dishwasher. The colored TV buying process was no exception. In his raspy, gruff voice, after years of daily heavy smoking and imbibing, P. and the old man went at it. Pop kept asking if he could get the first repair done for free because he had "heard" that Zenith TVs broke down a lot. P. went ballistic upon hearing such "rude rubbish" and told pop to go to hell and to visit Allen's, down the street. After calming down and having gone through a few Winstons, he and my dad reconciled and the sale was made, but not before more bickering and cuss words were exchanged within earshot of other customers. P. was a feisty and potty-mouthed haggler at heart, had little empathetic leanings and very few bedside manners. In his mind, the customer was always wrong! However, most of the locals knew and put up with him because he always delivered his merchandise on time, serviced his own products, and really didn't chisel anyone. So he had a few character flaws, so what. My dad and P. installed the state-of-the-art TV in our family room, plugged it in, adjusted the bunny ears, and made sure it fired up. There was no remote control, however. They shook hands and started laughing hysterically at their previous outrageous verbal brawl at his business and my mom joined in, speaking a few Russian words to him and making him laugh some more. P. left with our old set and mom opened the windows to air out the reeking cigarette smoke from the room; and we stood there, admiring the brand-new color television and hoping it would not break down any time soon. Because you know that would mean a call to P. and another drag-out verbal fight. You know, the norm. And one more thing: my sister and I had to sit at least ten feet away from the cathode ray tube because of the added x-rays that presumedly were emitted by color sets. We didn't want to get cancer from watching cigarette commercials on TV! Our viewing distance might have been justified and not just paranoia because eventually lead was added to the picture tube glass to reduce the supposedly "miniscule" emanating radiation levels. However, no one panicked, and television sales continued to grow. It was just like eating white Wonder Bread, nitrate infused bologna, and smoking Lucky Strikes in closed rooms. You know, the healthy norm in those ignorant days.

Home Life

I had recently turned 12 and we were living in a spacious, two-year old home (constructed over a three-year period by my father, paternal grandfather, a few subcontractors and me). I was being educated in a familiar school with familiar friends, and things on the surface seemed to be going swimmingly. Or, were they? I think they were, for the most part. But deep in the recesses of our family credo, be it my folks' immigrant status, or my very conservative, formerly persecuted and *old-fashioned* grandpa, an unfed beast groveled therein. There was this unspoken but palpable desire for my sister and I to somehow rise up and slay that hidden monster called mediocrity and become "important" people. Was it a European ideology? Was it my parents? And was it their well-meaning meanness that was meant to motivate me? I don't know but that's how I heard and felt it. Maybe I heard it wrongly? Anyway, I just wasn't good enough the way I was. Just being ME was a "failure." Contentment could only be had by great achievements in life. The future was to be espoused at the cost of the present. There were "big" things in store for me someday if only I worried, planned and obsessed about them on a daily basis. But I was only in seventh grade, darn it. Sure, I tried to live in the moment and no doubt developed a sense of humor as a coping mechanism, but the seemingly manufactured *heaviness* and mental browbeating was taking its toll on my fingernails. I was already a suspicious, observant and anxious kid, and the expectations at home merely compounded my hard-wired, nervous disposition. "What are you going to do with your life?" was a constant refrain from my father and Grandpa Pete. It was difficult coming up with non sarcastic replies to such a serious, yet ludicrous sounding question. My past academic and athletic performances meant nothing; they were barely passable to the harsh critics at home. It didn't help having a brilliant, civil engineer/college professor/superstar athlete/ handsome father. Or, a workaholic/can fix anything grandfather. At least Mom supported me and took my side, most of the time. I'm sure some of my classmates had similar haranguing experiences, but that didn't make it right. I retreated into my humor and bug worlds as needed, kept up a brave front in public, and saw my future as inevitably successful, however at a great cost to my psyche. Nevertheless, my naïve adolescent expectations and predictions bore fruit. Although I no longer bite my fingernails, the happiness, satisfaction and mental well-being assuredly "promised" me long ago, if I achieved x, y, and z, has thus far been elusive. However, along the way I have accumulated many material trinkets, a few vacation villas, a hot blonde wife, a lucrative dental career, and scholastically and athletically gifted children. Is that what life is all about on this insignificant dirt ball called earth in the middle of an unflinching and uncaring universe? Did I embody what I was preached? Or, did I simply get lucky? Also, what about my piece of mind? Am I truly enjoying all my perceived "successes" and fruits of my many labors or just going through the motions and continually balancing spinning plates in perpetuity? Perhaps I am ungrateful and should slap myself silly. And please don't tell me that my father was right all along!

28

Scholastic Scope

No more rinky-dink journalism for us junior high students; no more happy and sappy stories that the *Weekly Reader* had weekly instilled in we sixth graders last year. *Scholastic Scope*, the *radical*, weekly publication provided for free by our school in seventh-grade English class was edgy, insightful, "political" and seemingly age appropriate for 1971-72. The Vietnam War was raging, President Nixon was continually lying his butt off, the antiwar, women's rights and hippie movements were in full swing, the Kent State shootings had recently happened, and cyclamate was freshly banned from food in the U.S. Wow! There was a lot to digest and that seminal adolescent *print job* tried its best to inform us with satirical, poignant cartoons, insightfully well written news stories, and adverts that would appeal to our generation. And besides girls, boys had long hair too, and both sexes were shown wearing those blasphemous bell-bottoms in some of the magazine's pages. What was next, platform disco shoes and Elton John? Why yes, of course. The elementary school *Weekly Reader's* narration had been infantile drivel compared to the frequently "controversial" literature contained within *Scope*. The former sought to sooth and reassure, the latter to intimidate and agitate. I'm not sure why our school bothered to taunt the mostly "inbred" and farm bred students with progressive and left leaning ideology. It wasn't a communist rag, but you never knew whom it would affect and with what fervor. Maybe that was the whole point. I read it from cover to cover and laughed at some of the contrived and suggestive diatribes within. I quickly saw through the hyperbole and assumed that my classmates did as well. But it was a welcome addition nonetheless, a point of view that was decidedly different from the cloistered, stereotypical, and small-minded attitudes that most of the village idiots proudly professed. And as if on cue, Miss S., our young, bra-burning, feminist, male hating, seventh-grade English teacher/bitch nodded approvingly while commenting on every article in that magazine without qualifying or questioning some of the ulterior motives therein. It was all gospel to her and she preached its contents to us every week. Good ole' Miss S. and *Scope*; what a "liberal" and "lethal" combination they were. The song Robert Allen Zimmerman (aka Bob Dylan) once wrote, *The Times, They Are A-Changin'*, was still appropriate, even though written in 1964. I felt that it was truer than ever; things were rapidly changing, in the country and in our bovine-inspired, sometimes backward thinking school. Maybe Miss S. was right to rile up the offspring of dairy farmers and get them to consider more than cow teats and tractors? I often chuckled warmly at the juxtapositional absurdity of it all.

29

Those Blasted Ivories

Oh, sure, I still practiced daily, played publicly, and feigned enthusiasm for upcoming NYSSMA competitions. I was massaging the same old black and whites, and I was slowly burning out! Playing the piano was becoming more of a chore every day, yet I persisted because my ego was stroked by my mom and piano teacher, and I couldn't let them down. Or, could I? My third New York State School Music Association competition was approaching fast and my teacher was just barely wringing out what talent she could out of me. At least that's how it felt at the time. I appreciated the accolades but my lack of musicality started to derail an intoxicating and promising beginning when I was learning fast and furiously and, cockily showcasing my abilities at various venues around town, mostly at progressive Presbyterian church services. But now, by seventh grade, the writing was on the proverbial wall. I had musically hit a quagmire. Maybe it was the stress of being a pubertal adolescent, maybe Beethoven was bullshit, or maybe I really sucked and was being sucked along on this arduous keyboard journey by a teacher who wanted her *shekels* coming in regularly from my parents? All those thoughts were preventing me from exploring my true feelings for the piano, so I ended up doing what I always did in tense and terse situations: I doubled down and worked even harder to appease those around me and my own fragile sanity. I persevered like a butt nut until age sixteen, long after my fourth and final NYSSMA appearance in eighth grade. But, hey, I had received four perfect scores during those adjudications and that meant something, or did it? Realizing that I had reached the upper limit of my limited talent by my junior year, I finally retired from lessons and performances. A new teacher the year prior had failed to galvanize a positive response from my fingers even though the music selections had been provocatively modern and interesting to play. I was grateful for all the years of support I had received from family and friends but could not continue. Sadly, I quit. But like a retired ball player of any kind, I could and did play sporadically but now made more unforced errors as a result. I remember feeling special that piano was one of my "bags" early on in life, but lack of real talent rudely woke me up, so to speak, before I wasted any more perceived precious time and money on a "hobby" that would disappoint me in the end. However, I feel satisfied that I had achieved a slim margin of "success" as an elementary school and adolescent "piano man." And I continue to occasionally tickle the ivories on my black, Yamaha, baby grand, as needed. At least I can still scale those blasted keys!

30

Wrastlin'

I knew what all the farm boys in my gym class were waiting for. They mispronounced it with a country twang accent, but I knew what they meant. My PE teacher was the same one reamed out by my mom years earlier for giving me B grades for A-plus work. I liked gym and seemed to excel in all the sports offered thus far. I competed well against the future quarterbacks, running backs and point guards. I enjoyed being picked first for most sporty endeavors, either on the grassy playing field or indoors on the hard wooden floors. Although I still felt some discrimination from the teacher for being a brown-skinned and non local boy that frequently outshone his chosen stars, we begrudgingly got along. I never said boo to him. He never said much to me either. Good. "Today we are going to learn wrestling," said Mr. K. to much applause and catcalls from the cow tippers. At least HE pronounced the word correctly. We dutifully rolled out the protective rubberized mats and sat around in a large circle with him standing in the middle, with a whistle around his neck. Now, those haymongers weren't much at ball sports; some were woefully inept, clumsy and uncoordinated.

However, most were tall and strapping, used to hard work, and had calloused hands from milking stubborn udders. Shows of strength were what they were looking for and wrestling seemed like the perfect outlet for that. But what about gaunt boys like me? Sure, I could run and perhaps I should have run away. I played that "wussy sport" called tennis; I didn't relish getting a cauliflower ear or having my serving shoulder dislocated on a thin piece of foam. Plus, I wore glasses. I was in trouble. No wonder the mats were colored red. I imagined that none of my bloodletting would be noticed. Help! Using a favorite student, Mr. K. proceeded to demonstrate a few basic moves such as takedowns, reversals, riding, near falls, escapes, and mentioned the scoring system. Most of us already knew the sport having watched it at the collegiate level at our town's junior college, or on TV. "OK, first up, Izzy versus J.M.," announced Mr. K. I had known J.M since kindergarten. He was the prototypical junior jock: strong, handsome, blond, and blue-eyed, with a blossoming body that already could shoot, throw and catch at an above grade level. He probably brought back memories to Mr. K. when he was also a *jock-strap* at our same high school, years ago. But J.M. was not a bad dude. He was easy going and got along with everyone. Not a gentle giant but not a rub-it-in-your-face kind of athlete either. I liked him and maybe he also respected me, for I frequently bested him on the track in all distances. I removed my specs, we shook hands and began to grapple. Nothing pretty, mind you, just two boys trying to legally push, shove and hug one another for points. There was much yelling from the seated young men around us, mostly encouraging J.M., but I heard MY name mentioned a few times as well. After the obligatory three rounds, it was a stalemate in my mind, although J.M. had a few more takedowns of me. The whistle blew and Mr. K. raised my opponent's hand in victory. I was flushed, breathing hard and sore, just from that one measly and unskilled bout. The rough cut country *boyz* finally got their turns and I just sat there, amazed and enthralled by their brute power and killer instincts. I was glad that I already had my turn and was done, or was I? Mr. K. yelled that it was now time for the second go-round. Oh, no. How long were we going to keep at this floor rubbing sport? Although I greatly enjoyed being a spectator, I did not enjoy full immersion in it as a participant! "Izzy versus P.H.," Mr. K. blurted out. Shit! P.H., the huge and muscled farm boy, who was a klutz with a ball and known to run the wrong way on the track, bum-rushed me like a penned up raging bull at the sound of the whistle. He speared me and drove me to the mat knocking the wind out of me. Was this a WWE match or what? Oh, I had seen him coming, with his crouched and lowered shoulders and a devilish, combative look in his eyes, as if I was a skinny bullfighter waving a red flag. And then, while I was writhing and twitching on my back resembling a squashed bug, he proceeded to squeeze me like a python does while lying on top of me with all his weight. I got pinned and lay there lifeless as P.H. jumped up to many congratulations from his personal pals. Although victorious, he appeared sheepish looking and acted as though he never intended to hurt me. "Are you alright?" a stunned Mr. K. asked me. The whole match lasted fifteen seconds, tops. I didn't know what to say or do. I hurt all over as I managed to grunt a yes to his query and limped back to my seat next to my friends on the mat and put my specs back on my face. And at that very moment I suddenly realized that I was no *superman*; I was just Clark Kent with or without my glasses on, darn it. Although not a fan of mine, Mr. K. kept eyeballing me the rest of that class, probably to make sure I didn't barf, pass out or start crying in pain. And he made sure that he matched up the kids more equally as far as weight and musculature was concerned. I recovered and went on to win a few bouts myself in the ensuing weeks but I never faced P.H. again. I now had new respect for those gangly and unathletic ranch hands, masquerading as boys, in my class.

31

Hobbies and Passions

Junior high, namely seventh grade, was going, but going nowhere in my mind. Newly twelve, I was not flunking any particular course, but felt uncomfortable in many. My GPA was a low A, and though grateful for the classes that raised it, I felt unsure of myself and was mystified in the remaining ones, such as English, Math, Wood Shop, Agriculture, Art, and Music. History and Science, although tough courses with hard-marking teachers, seemed manageable and understandable to me. The others mentioned, not so much. School thus far was a hurried, puzzling affair, with a pesky locker mate, little time between classes, after school activities, long, morning bus rides, piles of homework, and parental units that briefly thought I was cut out for the prestigious and liberal Ivy League. Well, the names Harvard, Yale and Princeton were dropped a few times in my home, but then quickly forgotten about. However, in my own household, decades in the future, the exclusive Ivy League was not only frequently mentioned but gotten into by both my children. Of course, my headstrong and willful female child blew off Cornell in favor of McGill University (which is ranked higher than most Ivies) in Montreal, Canada, and my cerebral-assassin son dismissively declined both Cornell and Columbia in lieu of Brown. At least Brown University is an Ivy and it made me a proud papa. I had been involved in their college application processes and had tried my best as an unconnected, white, non legacy and monetarily non donating parent, and both children received the nod of admission to some of the best colleges in the world. But like a stupe, I paid all the costly tuitions, darn it. Maybe I had genetically and knowingly turned into that same, over-zealous, tiger parent that I formerly railed against years prior? But at least I wasn't just all talk like my old man was. I actually "walked the walk." But hopefully, I had been less than an overbearing bear, whenever scholastic ideas were bantered about in my own future household. Oh, well, back to 1972, again. Pop was relentlessly riding me as I flailed against the machinations of junior high; my grandpa Pete usually dismissed me as a flaky, lightweight, unfunny, wannabe jester with no future potential; Mom still loved me no matter what; and my sister looked up to me as an idyllic older brother. But what did she know? Fortunately for me, I had some hardcore hobbies and passions to buoy my spirits and body whenever I felt down and out, which was often in those dark days. Thank goodness I still had my insects, mudpuppies, bike riding, tennis, ping pong, piano, and violin to turn to in times of joy AND stress. Those seemingly obtuse and non related hobbies and passions of mine continued to occupy a large portion of my pea brain as I studied and suffered in that stultifying seventh grade. In addition, puberty was now upon me and greatly complicated matters, as previously non descript girls suddenly started to look *good*. I swam as hard as possible against the current of junior high but seemed to be caught in a perpetual riptide and mentally had to tread water to stay afloat. And forget about getting ahead! I frequently felt lost in the shuffle, no longer unique, no longer the lone witty wonder among the throngs of fellow students on the same mission as me. Luckily, I had a few close friends that I had bonded with and together we navigated our misfortunate year with humorous vigor and aplomb. There was no time for recriminations or regret. I constantly had to pull myself upright to take more fire from the teachers and try to learn something, while quietly laughing to myself at the ridiculousness of it all. My comic self was slowly coming back to life as I kept grinding away at that educational organ. It was the right thing to do, plus I had to pass into eighth grade, you know.

32

War

My parents were worried, but what else was new?
However, this time they had cause: the Vietnam War was
ongoing with seemingly no end in sight, and eventually I
might be drafted. I was 12, only six short years before being
eligible for the mandatory military service to fight those
damn "commie *gooks*." And I didn't say "comic books."
This was deadly serious, at least at my house. Fortunately,
futuristic planning was my family's forte and a cunning
ruse was slowly devised. My mom had a few immigrant
Estonian friends living in Toronto, right across the border
from our old haunts in western New York State and she
began writing them in Estonian "meaningful" letters about
my plight. Why Estonian? Well, one never knew if the FBI
or CIA were covertly opening and reading our mail, or not.
There were whispers even back then of our democratic
country snooping on private citizens. Maybe Nixonian-era
paranoia rubbed off on all of us at the time? But I'm sure
that our *deep state government* had Estonian translators
anyway, so any evasive linguistic maneuvers would have
probably just been childish annoyances to "them."
Anyhow, the plan for me to grow up Canadian and avoid

having to carry an M-16 or be carried home in a body bag never came to fruition because direct U.S. involvement ended the following year, with ALL hostilities over by 1975. And it turned out that many other boys had the same plan and some actually acted on it, and only came back to the U.S. as part of an American repatriation amnesty program issued by President Ford in 1974. But some stayed and became "Canucks" for life, eh? Nevertheless, my buddies and I were safe and got to stay home. My eventual northerly defection had fizzled by the war's abrupt ending in '73, but, meanwhile, 1972 and seventh grade raged on.

33

Entertaining Sports

There were no cable or satellite dishes back then, only the three basic TV networks and PBS. It was a pathetic serving of crap on most nights, even though we watched some of it on a regular basis. Our equally impoverished village had no movie theater, no watering holes (the town was *dry* at the time), no restaurants (the village diner, aka the *greasy* spoon, didn't count), and a recently boarded up bowling alley. Luckily the local two-year junior college up on the hill had healthy athletic programs with frequent games/ matches that were admission free to the villagers, should they wish to attend. It was great to take in regularly scheduled Division lll men's wrestling and basketball events, sometimes back to back on the same evening. On many a cold and snowy winter's night, THAT was usually the sole source of enjoyment for sports minded and entertainment starved townspeople like my family and me. Of course, we could have braved the other big hill in town and taken in the bevy of offered varsity high school sports. But the college ones were of a higher caliber, you know. Being a professor at said college, pop knew the sports schedule cold and we had the appropriate dates and times marked in bold ink on our usually blank calendar, hanging in our kitchen. The two big winter sports were men's wrestling and basketball. Women didn't wrestle collegiately at the time, although rumor had it that many females prolifically engaged in a form of it throughout the coed dormitories on our local campus. As for the women hoopsters, they were beyond bad. But while the male ball dribblers were also mediocre at the time, the wrestling team was nationally ranked, year after year, stocked with former state high school champions in almost every weight class. Why such talent at a relatively unheralded junior college? Well, the pugnacious wrestling coach and his program had developed a certain moxie reputation which fostered a winning culture over time. Plus, the college was relatively cheap to attend for two years. It then allowed talented sportsmen to transfer to a Division 1 wrestling program at a four-year university, which many of the grapplers did. Contrarily, although "blessed" with a former college standout, an NBA recruited player and now a stud of a coach, the men's basketball team was basically an underachieving program. And even though there were always a few talented, local, high school graduates on the undersized squad, they never made an impactful difference. So, on many a wintry Friday night, my family, including Grandpa Pete, who loved watching wrestling, would file into the college gymnasium along with throngs of fellow techies and townies alike, climb the wooden bleachers, shed our goose down coats and settle in for the wrestling extravaganza. It was always a spectacle. The opposing mat-men knew they would lose badly and glumly put up with the ostentatious light show, the spirited introductions and heady display of machismo and posturing from our home team. And then those visitors would get beaten to a pulp. Oftentimes, the basketball game would follow, so we frequently received a double header of testosterone fueled sports. The visiting basketball team would often take out their losing wrestling team's frustrations on our *home boys* and wallop them, running up the score and showing no mercy. Our frantically waving and gesticulating head coach was usually visibly apoplectic due to the booing public. But, hey, it was free admission, so we didn't really care THAT much. Anyway, just a brief aside to this story: the basketball coach had asked my old man (who was also the college men's tennis coach and top player in our town) to teach him tennis and he did. They developed a "jock's camaraderie" and guess what, the thirty-something year-old basketball whiz ended up a fantastic tennis player, even beating my father just before he left for SUNY Oswego's basketball program, in the usual stepping stone routine found in the coaching world. My pop was not pleased at losing to M.D., but at the same time marveled at his fitness, athleticism and quick learning ability. Anyhow, those days watching something besides TV were wonderful although I'm not sure if my mom and sister really appreciated the nuances of a half nelson, a near fall, a take down or a technical foul. But I did.

Ski Bums

Ski bums? Well, not really. However, as my sister and I grew older my family progressed from wintry activities such as tubing, tobogganing and sledding to skiing. Well, not REAL downhill skiing, but *boring* and most pedestrian, cross-country skiing. But, hey, we were on the snow, shushing up and down hills and dales while frantically planting our poles to keep balanced and moving forward. The "rich" and wannabe wealthy people in town downhill skied, the rest of us stayed within our middle-class lane and cross-country tracks, and plodded along, pretending we were actually skiing. Of course, those were the early days, before cross-country skiing exploded onto the national and world scene with better techniques, better equipment and better competition. Olympic cross-country races became as awesome to view as the downhill events. But for we '70s "pole planters," and particularly MY family, our sojourns in our backyard and later the local college golf course were devoid of lift tickets, mountain club fees, the requisite pricey dining out and "free" hot chocolate in the heated and opulent ski lodges where supposedly *hot* snow bunnies perpetually hung out. At least that's what I heard the experience was like from friends who REALLY skied. MY experience was: getting out of a cold car, waxing the ski bottoms with the correct wax, toeing my ice cold cross-country boots into the three holes in the bindings, snapping the bindings shut, looking out at the familiar golf course terrain in front of me while being pummeled by a wicked snowstorm and slowly following a barely visible already made trail, pushing my poles in as needed to keep going, and silently complaining about my freezing toes! We never had any formal lessons, just common sense and a sense of equilibrium. Even my super athletic old man was a beginner at something! But we did possess top of the line equipment: Fischer brand skis, poles, boots, gators and bindings. At least we looked good from a distance. All of our *walks* were devoid of frills and thrills but were essentially free. However, there was no hot chocolate to look forward to and no gorgeous babes on the course, just a few bundled up diehards and my family. If you wanted to rest, you just stopped. If you wanted a drink, you drank ice cold water from a metal canteen strapped to your waist. No wine, of course. And no whining! However, it was mostly "fun," and you worked up a quick lather in no time flat. Layers of clothing were shed as needed to keep from overheating if you kept up a fast clip. I did not play winter tennis and since I did not play high school basketball or wrestle, indoor table tennis and cross-country skiing were my active sports during those long ago, frosty, and snowy winters. Cavorting, falling and flailing our poles around gave my family and me a smattering of exertion during our skiing excursions. I surmised it was probably more exercise than most people engaged in during that time era. Riding around on a Moto-Ski or Ski-Doo snowmobile was obviously more exhilarating but most likely free of actual movement of arms and legs, unless you were stupid or drunk and had an accident, which was a fairly common occurrence in our area. However, many was the time that I would enviously look at friends in the distance riding a Polaris or Arctic Cat while I was crushing my quadriceps, hamstrings and triceps while allegedly "skiing." Oh, well, we would arrive home, tired, hot, sweat soaked, and became quickly surrounded by wet clothing and garments strewn around the family room. Our faces were flushed, our ears were red, and we were all fatigued, but smiled nonetheless. It must have been the endorphin rush. Although not a ski bum, I guess I did enjoy our primitive attempts at a great sport without the outlay of much money back in those days. Today, I have basically morphed from cross-country skiing to snowshoeing, who some say is an even "lazier" way to traverse snow covered ground. However, I have been a four-time international snowshoe sprint champion, having won the 100 and 200-meter races in consecutive years using Dion custom made snowshoes from Vermont. I struck gold in Lewiston, Maine and in Gatineau, Canada. I retired from competitive sprinting years ago and now snowshoe for fun and relaxation, but sometimes showboat a little with a quick sprint or two, just to show off for any onlookers! Winter fun these days is weather permitting: that means when we have snow, which has become somewhat of a scarce commodity lately.

35

The Victory Garden?

I know, it is an old slogan from World War ll days, when U.S. citizens were encouraged to supplement government enforced food rationing by planting fruit and vegetable gardens to help ensure their nutritional needs. The word Victory was probably facetiously added to not only thumb our proverbial noses at the Nazis, but to provide much needed positive propaganda at the home front. The "program" had rational roots and worked for the betterment of Americans till the war's end. So, is that why my paternal grandpa Pete planted and "religiously" managed a quarter-acre garden plot on our south-facing, flat, terraced hill just behind our house? He didn't see any soldierly action during the war, he and his immediate family were literally running for their lives from the Russian communists and then from the invading Krauts! But once in this country, and after a twenty-plus year career working as a mechanic at J.H. Williams and Co. in western N.Y., he must have found his Estonian farmer roots once again. Since 1967 he lived with my immediate family in our sleepy town where mom stayed home and my father was employed as a professor at the local junior

college. After a rough beginning, with a few stints in rental
housing on Clinton Street before we built our own home,
Grandpa finally settled in. He was a formerly wealthy
Estonian landowner back in his prime and perhaps peering
out over a large, "useless," mowed, lawn got his juices
flowing again? Maybe it was the unfamiliar purple colored
soil and the endless rocks that challenged him, as well?
Anyway, he finally went completely bananas in the spring
of 1972, greatly expanding our previously "normal-sized"
village garden by furiously planting raspberry bushes,
current bushes, plum, apple and pear trees, and endless
rows of corn and potatoes for the first time. He even stuck
a hazelnut seedling into the dirt, next to his newly built,
concrete-blocked, green, painted shed. What was going on?
The Vietnam War did not "require" us Americans to plant
a garden! "Tricky Dick" Nixon had not made any such
pious proclamations. It was silly. My father earned enough
dough to keep us well fed; what was really going on? Was it
boredom, workaholism and wanting to feel needed? Was it
his own version of "victory" over previous persecutorial
adversity? I surmise it was most of the above. My younger
sister and I were given more than an inkling by the
self-appointed *Hetman* (ancient tribal leader in Eastern
Europe) that we should not only be eternally grateful for
all his upcoming hard work and agricultural acumen, but

should enthusiastically be ready to "help out" at a moment's notice. Yeah, right. It was only spring, the shoots were just barely sprouting, and already the family "General" was giving orders. I was also busy planning a busy spring/summer of swimming, insect collecting, bike riding, and tennis; my sister probably had her own agenda. So, I was wary when Grandpa Pete not so subtly insinuated that the summer of '72 would be the summer of stone picking, *hoeing*, insect pest eradication, *hoeing*, watering, *hoeing*, and then maybe harvesting. He emphatically stated, in Estonian, that he was fed up with "amateur hour" and was finally serious about growing veggies again. Holy crap. What was he before? Were we back in rural Estonia again? Did he also buy some horses and plows when we weren't looking? My old man would shortly be shuffling off to summer school for his second, specialized three-month circuit at RIT, enroute to garnering a master's degree as decreed by his college's engineering department. Mother would be gardening later, mainly as an unwilling but cooperative family member toeing the line, to can and freeze the anticipated bonanza. That left my sister and me to do the grunt work, to be the migrant workers, the free slave labor on our "farm." We were involuntarily conscripted to be the rock removers, insect killers, berry pickers, soil tillers, weed whackers, fertilizer appliers, and all-around garden scut-monkeys. We would be hunched over in the sweltering sun squashing Colorado potato beetle larvae or picking stones while Grandpa happily sat in his opened shed, shooting unwanted birds away with his trusty homemade slingshot. Small pebbles would go zinging over our heads, but we never got hit. He was a good shot. Obviously Grandpa Pete did the heavy lifting in that giant dirt patch, from morning till night, from spring until fall, besides fixing things around the house as needed. But we youngsters were always supposed to be on standby, on call. I had to frequently and sneakily get away early to ride my five-speed Scwhinn, chase butterflies or catch some salamanders. But there was always that look of disappointment and anger from Grandpa when I returned home. Many was the time when my father had to put his foot down for us to play tennis or to go hunting or fishing together. I learned to avoid that darn garden whenever possible. It may have been a victory for my obsessed grandfather but was a chore-filled, miserable experience for me. Nevertheless, pop came home in late summer and I was truly elated. We began tasting the fruits of our labors come autumn and had saved a buck or two on leafy produce, in the process. Plus it was all organic, except for the Rotenone that was used on the potato plants. Nonetheless we were made aware in no uncertain terms of my grandfather's hard labors between bites of corn and squash at many suppers. Today, as a certified master gardener myself, I have had bountiful gardens my entire adult life and appreciate the sometime back-breaking work that goes into managing them. But I believe it should be a hobby AND a labor of love for the entire family, especially a non farming one. Again, I never really minded the work required to earn the fresh fruit and excellent tasting vegetables that yearly graced our home all those years ago. But I did mind being constantly reminded of my grandfather's "sacrifices" and toil to feed us alleged woebegone waifs, especially since mom, sis and I did so much of the drudgery. And we definitely were not starving.

36

Vietnam

Seventh grade English, with our school's resident *feminazi*, firebrand teacher Miss S., was more than a class about novel literature. In fact, it was much, much more. She sardonically discussed religions, politics, women's rights, and male chauvinism as easily as adolescent appropriate poetry. Sometimes she combined the two. On this one occasion, we were told to team up in twosomes, research a relatively recent newsworthy topic, write a short paper on it and be prepared to give a brief oration with a question and answer type format. Are you kidding me? Were we supposed to give a live press conference, too? Were we going to testify in front of the U.S. senate judiciary committee? Obviously, Miss S. had been watching way too much Pentagon Papers drama on TV! Holy crow, that was a lot to do for one measly report. But she gave us specific guidelines and various media hints for what she expected, and we proceeded – Tally Ho! I quickly selected J.N. as my partner in crime. We went way back to elementary school and had participated quite successfully in group assignments as a dynamic duo. Firstly, we had to carefully select a subject. I know, the Vietnam War. Other fellow students picked newsy themes such as Nixon's historic meeting with China's Chairman Mao, the space-launch of Pioneer 10, Equal Rights Amendment issues, Badfinger's latest album, etc. But WE stuck to the war because Miss S. seemed to know so much about it. As lowly males, this was going to be a no-brainer, to ingratiate ourselves on her and get a high mark as well. Yeah, baby! Well, WE ended up the no-brainers in the end. Who knew that she was in fact THAT knowledgeable and suspicious of our government's involvement in that southeast Asia debacle, and who knew that the nascent Pentagon Papers would reveal the Johnson administration's outright deceit of the American people about the Vietnam War effort? She may have also been a conspiracy theorist, and none would have blamed her in those tumultuous times. But WE didn't understand her innermost vehement feelings at that point. We had an inkling but did not realize the depth of her demented depravity concerning all things patriarchal, which included the war! J.N. and I were seventh graders, slightly politically informed but basically naïve as hell about most adult things. We were only 12 years old, dammit, as we began the hunting and foraging process as clueless clods. We had a few weeks to gather info, materials, and then present our paper before giving the presentation. And here is where we made our biggest faux pas. Instead of gathering the intel

and writing our piece as a countercultural dissertation, we
"mistakenly" took the government's side, the side that news
anchor Walter Cronkite nightly implored us to take; the
side of U.S. "victory," secretive but willful treachery, and
sloppy sloganism such as "Peace with Honor," as DICK
Nixon would later ruefully utter. If only we had "agreed"
with Miss S.'s ideas we would have been golden, but it
didn't happen. We wrongfully assumed that it was a minor
English project, plus most of the available "war stuff" was
pro-government slanted. Additionally, we didn't have
access to very much tangible anti-war rhetoric besides her
unquotable tyrannical rants and the hippie histrionics in
the news. So, with a school AV department-issued
primitive tape recorder in hand, J.N. and I were excused
during lunch to go into town and interview some locals
about their opinions on the war. We questioned, recorded,
took copious notes, read books, articles and listened
intently to the *CBS Evening News*. After handing in our
jointly hand-written one-page masterpiece (I actually wrote
it), it was now our turn to spill our guts in front of a live
studio audience. J.N. was up first; he played and explained
our mostly pro-war interviews, outlined our discussion,
mentioned the Viet Cong, and gave a very detailed account
of the lead up to the major battles that followed. So far, so
good. Miss S. just sat there glumly, looking rather bored. I

was up next. I spoke clearly, detailing the minutia of the war itself, the politics involved, and its consequences to our country and the two Vietnams, thus far. And that's when the witch's fangs came out. Miss S. abruptly stood up and proceeded to unfairly criticize me and used profane language to demean what I had said. She proceeded to tell the class that I was wrong on almost all accounts and then screamed for us all to wake up, wise up and not trust the government. Then she angrily asked me politically charged questions that I could not answer. I stammered and stuttered with futile answers that incensed her even more. She glared at me as if I had violated all the principles she dearly stood for. I had been hoping for an easy A, and now hoped for a C, if possible. Crap. Mercifully, there were no questions for J.N and I from the tight-lipped peanut gallery as we sat down, red-faced, embarrassed, and spent. Definitely no Brownie points that day! We both received a B grade for our juvenile effort, written next to the red ink splashed liberally across our handed-in "piece of shit." Not bad, but not good, either. Anyway, that disastrous episode in seventh-grade English pales in comparison to the life and early death of eighteen-year-old high school alumnus, PFC Richard Earl S., who made the ultimate sacrifice during the Vietnam War, in 1968. I vividly recall walking daily past his placard, which was prominently displayed in our school's front lobby, seeing his face, and then thinking of what grievances Miss S. harbored against that war and contempt for all things male. She may have been correct on some matters and politically savvy on many accounts, but her lack of civility and empathy irked me to no end. Richard Earl. S. was deceased, and she could not bring him back, regardless of her pompous ravings and elitist "moral" code.

37

Bats in the Belfry?

After suffering through two successive quarters of mandatory "manly" courses (Agriculture and Wood Shop) for boys, it was finally time for me to relax with something completely different, something I knew a lot about: music. But hold on there, *Mozart*, this course would not turn out to be as easy as I had vividly imagined it would. The first day turned into the best day in that damned classroom, much to my surprise and ire. It was the last period of the afternoon as I slowly sauntered in and, instantly noticed that it was a coed class. So far, so good. F., E.G. and I settled comfortably into some back row seats, chattering and kidding around while awaiting the teacher's arrival. We were fast friends at this point and took every opportunity to socialize, be it in study halls, orchestral rehearsals, the lunch room, the hallways, or now in music class! How hard could this musical endeavor be? My immediate pals and I already knew our notes because of violin lessons; plus years of piano instruction had taught me theory as well. I wasn't worried. And, besides, I was already well acquainted with the teacher. She was the middle-aged, unmarried daughter of my elderly, entomological, "patron saint," the retired

Presbyterian minister that had sought to bolster my knowledge of all things buggy when I was growing up on his street. So, I conceitedly leaned my head against the back wall and smiled, knowing that I would handily ace this daily "waste of time." Ha, ha. The joke was on me. In stormed Miss R. like a storm trooper and proceeded to yell and scream for us to quiet down. I sat up quickly and struggled to recall her being so overtly brusque and rude. We had interacted many times at her father's house and she had always been pleasant, soft spoken and demure. In the classroom she seemed to turn into a hellish beast, hellbent on teaching we dummies music, whether we liked it or not. I was still in a state of shock at her "bipolar" demeanor when she spied me in the back row, giving me a nod and a wink. But then she proceeded to sternly lecture my bewildered classmates on deportment and respect. I guess it was needed, because nobody really wanted to behave in a "joke period" just before dismissal, including me. But she did have the chops and wherewithal to accomplish her teacherly tasks. She was sturdily stocky, quirky, with numerous facial tics, and a pitch-perfect voice that could knock you down. A talented pianist and singer, she quickly had the class subdued with her loud mouth, and in short order had us wishing the scholastic quarter was over, so we could move on to art. And that was on the first day of class, the good day! The rest of the quarter was filled with dread; it was an endless barrage of note taking, forced singing, exams, quizzes and a "term" paper at the end. WTF? This was music class, not a science course. Eighth period became drudgery as pupils would gloomily file in, take their seats with no talking, whip out notebooks and begin frantically copying her copious chalkboard scribbling. I could hardly make out the miniscule writing but clearly heard her every word, loud and clear. After twenty minutes or so of expounding on musical history and theory, she would abruptly drop her chalk and start pounding on the piano in the corner, cajoling us to sing along. She slammed the ivories, while the piano shuddered and shook, barely able to stand upright. Miss R. was a blustery babe that took her vocation way too seriously, especially for junior high. Anyway, she and I got along, and I managed to do well in that boisterous classroom, in spite of her histrionics and endless babbling. And, as an added bonus, I also auditioned for my first high school operetta, which she was solely in charge of. It was a yearly undertaking, along with the annual school play. I was terrible at singing but there were multiple minor speaking parts available and I snagged one, as a seventh grader! I think there was favoritism involved but I needed the Brownie points anyway, to keep my average high.

Nevertheless, I had scored a paltry part in the upcoming school musical and kept putting up with her tyrannical ways, which continued unabated while she fiercely directed we "talentless artistes" at multiple ensuing rehearsals. Whatever made me think she was a nice, levelheaded person in the first place? She was nothing like her father, or was she? I had never received an official godly sermon from him, filled with fire and brimstone, so maybe there was some genetic continuity and similarity? However, was it instead just a carefully crafted classroom act? She was so genial outside of class and a bully in it. Was she genuinely angry or not? I had no one to ask and never found out. As a family friend and former neighbor, my folks thought the world of her and didn't believe a single derogatory allegation that I had inferred. I should have tape-recorded the typical class balderdash, but did not. Oh, well. Anyhow, I escaped that quarter of batty music unscathed, with an A average, and was truly grateful. Miss R. also taught eighth grade music the following year, and that course I almost blew!

38

Creamy Goodness

Our town was literally immersed in milk; a myriad of active dairy farms ringed our rural settlement in all directions. Yet, when it came time for us non farmers and village dwellers to procure various milk concoctions, we were not offered the locally made stuff. We purchased butter, cheese, ice cream and milk that was pasteurized and homogenized in other parts of the state and country. The nearby Dellwood creamery, in a very small hamlet a few miles past our town, bought most of our locale's raw milk but sold the resultant products to stores in New Jersey. But, why? Instead of the locals benefitting from happy and contented local cows, we got white dairy sludge and other milky merchandise from nebulous farms from who knows where? Sure, our native farmers drank and ate their own output, but what about the rest of us? I guessed the local creamery got paid substantially more by stores elsewhere and we townspeople got the *foreign made*, store-bought dregs instead. So what my mom and other housewives did early on was to befriend a few farming families and bought unpasteurized and unblended milk directly from the tap, so to speak. She also purchased farm fresh eggs, bacon, and sides of beef and pork before the words *farm-to-table* and *organic* were in vogue. It was cash-and-carry, you know. After bringing home the four or five, glass, gallon jars full of natural milk, she would boil said liquid and let it cool before letting us have a drink. We never got sick while consuming that high fat compound, and none of us were overweight in the '70s. Just sayin.' And as far as I could tell, there was no real animosity toward the creamery for gipping we villagers out of locally made articles. Firstly, it employed a large cadre of local yokels and, secondly, it had a dinky outlet store by the roadway, where townsfolk could at least buy ice cream containers and servings that were made from "our own milk!" The prices were a few pennies more than the artificially flavored Sealtest shit peddled at the Grand Union on Main Street and by our blind neighbor Bruce H., but was definitely worth the car ride to go and get it. Many warm, spring, Sunday afternoons were leisurely spent by my family and me taking a station wagon automobile ride to the "real" country to obtain "real" ice cream. It was only a five-mile trip, but felt much longer, along a winding and little traveled county highway. My sister would usually have a double pecan cone and I a triple maple walnut. Pop had his plain vanilla and Mom her usual favorite, chocolate. We would sit in the small dirt parking lot for a while, savoring and licking the creamy goodness clutched in our hands while knowingly nodding to other families that were present. And my folks would always invariably remark about how fortunate we were to be living in such a beautiful and bountiful area. Now, we assumed that the ice cream was all natural. I mean, we could see the creamery and its billowing smokestack in the distance. But who knew about things like that back then? Only the MILK may have been genuine, with the cream-filled wafer cones full of deleterious "poisons" that was perfectly legal in those days. Nothing was labeled, and nobody asked any questions. Did the ice cream also contain polysorbate 80, diglycerides and guar gum like the Hood-brand cartons that were sold at the Victory supermarket in town? Was Nixon really a crook? Were we simply naïve and overly trusting? Probably, but most people were at the time. Nevertheless, we would have our cold, sugary treats and drive back home, satiated and happy about the bucolic excursion we had just been on. Some of those long-ago days were truly free of stress, at least to an anxious and worrywart twelve-year-old like me. Maybe they were also full of saccharin instead of natural sucrose, but free of stress nonetheless.

39

The Biking Caravan

It was a sight to behold, roughly twenty adolescent riders on all shapes and sizes of bikes, furiously peddling and sandwiched between my parents at either end. But it wasn't planned or even sanctioned by the two adults present. So, how did those spontaneous bike rides coalesce, expand, and happen in the first place? Once in a while on warm spring evenings, my folks would whip out their two-wheelers and cajole my younger sister and me to join them for an outing on the backroads of our town; roadways that were usually devoid of heavy traffic. What a treat it was. Sure, I had ridden my trusty, golden, five-speed Schwinn a gazillion times on Clinton Street, by myself or with my sis, but these were extra special times because mom and dad were with us. However, what began as a nuclear family affair quickly turned into an explosion of additional riders that magically glommed on to us as we rode through various neighborhoods. Unchaperoned children of all ages that were already out peddle-pushing must have seen my folks and figured that they could safely tag along because grownups were in their midst. I didn't recognize or know any of those kids! My parents reluctantly acquiesced and let new cyclists join our burgeoning band of ragtag riders. Of course, there were no-hold harmless or non disclosure forms to sign back then, but maybe there should have been. Mom and dad became patsies, glorified babysitters, over and over again. What the hell? They became unwitting and unwilling stooges responsible for a bunch of youngsters because they couldn't say no. Many kinds of accidents could have befallen the motley crew during our riding jaunts and my family would have undoubtedly been blamed. Fortunately, none occurred, not even a flat tire. And, as usual back then, nobody wore helmets or any protective or reflective attire. We had gotten lucky. Anyway, we stopped doing the "caravan" thing after the ludicrous line of bikers became so long as to constitute a danger to themselves and a hazard for automobile drivers. My pop put away his Raleigh ten-speed (which he proudly bestowed on me the following year) and my sister and I would only cycle solo, on selected streets, away from the mobs that sought us out. However, all those wonderful prior excursions taught me not only the layout of the town streets but the rural highways meandering through scenic hills and dales as well. The following summer, when my dad was at Rochester Institute of Technology, completing his master's program, I would frequently bolt away from my workaholic paternal grandpa on that vintage Raleigh and speedily traverse our village and outlying areas to my heart's content. I guess all those previous biking treks had given me the confidence to strike out on my own, to help me escape the endless drudgery and "work" that always awaited me back home upon my return. I still have that beautiful bike, somewhere.

40

The Yorker Club

Whether it was an officially sanctioned scholastic club found throughout New York state high schools or uniquely dreamed up by our seventh-grade history teacher, I did not know at the time. He was new, we were new, and junior high was new…. Who knew? Anyway, a few months into the year our beloved instructor organized an afterschool program called the Yorker Club. It would investigate and emphasize New York state Native American and colonial cultures, ancient anecdotes and artifacts from our state as well as engage in hands-on project making and limited field trips. As far as I could tell it was a continuation of our normal daytime history class, but with more in-depth discussion and elaboration. Although not truly a history buff, how could I resist signing up when most of my classmates so willingly and eagerly did? Mr. K., a true history maven, made a compelling case for the club and there I found myself, sitting in the school auditorium's front row with most of my cohorts around me, listening intently and imaginatively as Mr. K. spun and weaved yarn after yarn in quick succession. We were all hopelessly *addicted*, me included. Hooked yes, but hopefully not snookered into having joined a "cult." I was always slightly paranoid about being a joiner, and still am. But I instinctively trusted the teacher and had no qualms or trepidations about his motives. The club was supposedly open to all high school students; however, as I surveyed the surrounding scurvy lot, only seventh grade faces were seen. It was that brand new! The meetings were supposed to be weekly, then monthly, then whenever. It was hard to gather students on a regular basis with sports and other agendas jammed in their schedules. However, when present, we earnestly listened to Mr. K. And we went on a few trips, such as to the local historical society's farmer's museum featuring my burgeoning BFF's founding village forefather and we undoubtedly learned local village folklore along the way. We sang Haudenosaunee (Iroquois) chants, played early Dutch games, handled antique British muskets, 19th century glass bottles and archaic carpenter's tools that I shared (after finding them on my property before our new house was built). One of the last significant meetings, in the spring of '72, was a real pip. Mr. K. implored us to bring boots that day as we were going to go for a short hike behind our alma mater, right after school dismissal. We club members assembled in a disarrayed queue in back of our school building as Mr. K. took his spot in the lead and off we marched into the adjoining hill, our winter galoshes squishing and squashing with each mucky step. We were clueless as to what we would be doing a mere thirty paces from the school. The only hint he dropped was that the formerly local Delaware Indians of yesteryear used to do it too. Do what??!! Why, look for nourishing leeks, what else? What??!! Our fearless *chieftain* shuffled through the remaining snow and leaf litter and quickly found his prize: a leek plant. Wild leeks are "mild" members of the garlic/onion family and rise early from the earth, sprouting in early spring in patches, and in wooded areas. Our teacher soiled his hands by pulling one up, wiped off the dirty detritus on his pants, and took a big bite out of the white stem part, just below the green, floppy leaf tops. We just stood and stared at him as he chewed, swallowed and grinned, remarking, "Crispy, just right!" So, we fellow Yorkers began rooting around ourselves, finding and uprooting the succulent, naturally found allium vegetables. Nobody got sick, but in fairness, no one, including me, really had more than a few tepid nibbles each. I and most students took some cleaned off plants home for our parents and siblings to enjoy. Mom said they were plain old wild onions and was nonplussed as to the fuss I made over the few wilted offerings I reverently presented to her. I had to correct her; what did parents, know, right? The Yorker Club ended shortly thereafter, prior to the close of the

school year. The club even got its photo in the yearbook
that year. It had been an adventurous hoot. Although it
evolved into a hugely popular club, with high schoolers of
all ages participating in it during ensuing years, and
becoming part of a large New York State annual
convention series, I quit after that one year of belonging.
Piano, violin, operettas, tennis and ping pong lessons,
besides nightly studying, consumed my eighth-grade time
and I could not serve yet another master, try as I might.
But it had been a wonderful time, with a wonderful
teacher and, yes, his wondrous stories. Thanks, Ed.

41

Artistically Declined

Another eighth period quarter of mandatory malarkey was up to bat, this time, art. The previous quarter of coed music with that bombastic, shrill and daft Miss R. had thankfully ended. I was somewhat of an accomplished musician (mainly piano, not the violin) but had a bewildering time in that daffy music course, comprehended virtually nothing, and only pretended to listen and behave because of an out of school bond with the teacher's father, my entomological mentor. Yes, I was selected to be in the annual school operetta due to favoritism on her part, but insisted on a non vocal role, which I received. Anyway, I took my low A final grade from her and got geared up for art. The art room was basically two large classrooms joined together at the end of the hall on the second floor. There was enough space in there to house ceramic kilns, tons of art supplies, spacious desks, and there was room to roam. Middle-aged Mr. L. was our resident Salvador Dali type. He was a long haired, curly maned and heavily mustachioed *gaucho*, with a devilish glint in his eye, and with a sarcastic retort to most questions. He fancied himself a true artiste' and played the part to perfection, if only at the unappreciated high school level. His wife had been our grammar school art instructress in grades K-6 but did not embody the same farcical, "artistic" affectations as he did. He swayed, he gestured, he sauntered, he entertained and criticized, and it was only the first ten minutes of class, as I meekly sat still and stared. I considered myself to be an above average drawer, sketcher and painter, and most of my peers had knowingly "approved" of my artwork as we slowly evolved through the elementary grades. I had always scored highly on art pieces and usually received compliments for my efforts. Even working with clay did not flummox me, and without taking risks I usually turned out porcelain products without cracks in them. Although I was initially in awe of the buffoonish Mr. L., I felt confident that all my ensuing *creativity* would be enough for an easy A. I was wrong. No matter what I drew or outlined or in whatever medium, he was not happy. Didn't he get the memo? Didn't his wife ever mention my name as an up and coming, gifted, artist? Did they live together? Anyway, he always gave me that disappointed smirk of disgust as if I had just handed him a fresh booger or some soiled toilet paper to gaze at. Secondly, he had trouble pronouncing my surname. And then, while already pushing a B average, I further aggravated him. He was up at the front, lightly

sketching an anatomically correct male on the blackboard
when he asked if anyone knew what the curved bottom
bones at the base of the spine were called. Having read and
absorbed many age appropriate anatomy texts thus far in
my spare time as well as having glued together plastic
see-through miniature human models, I felt confident
about the hominid form and body. I piped up that the
answer he was looking for was the scrotum. Classmates
turned their heads toward me and nodded in unison. Most
assumed that I obviously knew the right rejoinder because
of my "scientific proclivities." Well, I was wrong as Mr. L.'s
face turned a deep red while he loudly pronounced that the
correct answer was the coccyx. I slunk down in my chair.
What had made me say the word scrotum? I knew what
the right response was. What was wrong with me? Mr. L.
glared at me for a long time, invariably thinking that I was
a wise-ass jerk trying to embarrass him or to at least get a
rise out of the class. He already "hated my talentless
talent," my name, and now most likely thought I was
goofing on him, too. But it wasn't on purpose, I tell you. It
just happened to slip out. I was mortified beyond belief at
my faux pas. Anyhow, the remainder of the course was
horrible for me. I felt vilified, degraded and thwarted at
every turn and began to despise being there, with that
pompous prick pontificating principles of art that I already

knew. As a gifted artist himself, my dad thought that some of my tommyrot was actually decent and laughed at my misery. The course ended, Mr. L. entered my final quarterly grade in my report card and guess what? I had garnered an A for the marking period. How, and why? Maybe my *trashy* renderings were not that bad after all? Perhaps the teacher had smartly sought to get more out of me the whole time with a toxic but planned mixture of demeaning and depressing diatribes? Mr. L. malevolently winked at me as his dancing eyes twinkled and said, "See you in eighth-grade art, putz." It was an insulting play on my last name and I hated being called that, but an A was an A and I took it like a man, or, at least, a twelve-year-old *putz.*

42

Expectations

We have touched on this touchy subject before. However, I feel it is worth revisiting because many of my buds not only felt MY pain growing up, they also unwillingly participated in their own unbeknownst family angst and dramas. I only knew about others' alleged kin related misfortunes because some of my closest pals spilled the beans to me. So, what was it about some parents and their offspring in the '70s? I don't claim to be a shrink or psychologist (maybe just a psycho?) but was observant enough to know that a few of my chums and I had similar mentally rough upbringings, with unrealistic expectations heaped upon us at birth. It reminds me of the 1955 Disney classic *Lady and the Tramp*, when Jim Dear, the snobby father figure, hurriedly and presumptuously attaches a Yale pennant over the crib of his unborn son as if getting accepted to and graduating from that college would be a mere formality. Of course things were a bit different in 1910, the time period in the movie, before affirmative action, mandatory female enrollment, the Asian student Ivy onslaught, and Yale's current 5% admit rate. But like today, I'm sure 1910 also had its share of American "wealthy

150

elites" (Jim Dear) whose children were magically and methodically granted admission to the storied Ivies regardless of talent or brains. My prep school class valedictorian, super athletic, overqualified, and legally blind son was denied admittance to Yale in 2010. Fortunately, Cornell, Columbia and Brown universities had just enough *minority*, "white male," middle class seats remaining to offer him Ivy League enrollment. And, a snobby Brown banner continues to hang on the wall next to HIS bed in his old bedroom. And later, after graduating from a top ten law school, he turned out just fine, I think. But did I also heap unrealistic expectations on my own son? Do you reap as you heap? Was I a pushy, conceited, asshole parent that plainly got lucky that my progeny stepped up to the plate and homered? Probably. Now, back to MY sob story. As previously mentioned, starting at a young age, unrealistic expectations hit many of my friends and me hard. It was initially a tough slog in junior high, negotiating the academic processes, furtively trying to obtain high grades, and putting up with sprouting puberty while being upbraided at home for not measuring up. My folks wanted me to get ahead; ahead of what, I don't rightly know. My father was a white-collar college professor and "drove the bus" as far as belittling me into supposed positivity. Was that the pop-psychology back then? Using derisive comments and criticisms to cajole and motivate your offspring? Well, that was the norm in my household. At least that was my interpretation of the subconscious mind games that were being played, with me being the perpetual patsy. But I wouldn't have minded if I also had received clear, unambiguous signals and real guidance from the male chiefs. Instead, I was given nebulous expectations to fulfill without a realistic game plan or academic map to follow and was "expected" to become a civil engineer, like pop, or a doctor. I was in seventh grade and had my future basically planned out for me, however, nobody actually stepped up to help me make that eventuality come true. I was supposed to magically wake up one morning as an engineer or a doctor and make everyone proud and happy. It was a horrible feeling having to constantly field questions about my futuristic career when I was busy stumbling in seventh-grade math! My anxiety was through the roof. I was supposed to do the right things and have my career path down pat at 12 years of age. Are you kidding me? But that's how my family functioned, or should I say dysfunctioned. My stay-at-home mom at the time was of no help, my grandpa Pete was an overbearing, *old-world* ogre, and my father was always conveniently "missing in action" whenever it was crunch time to assist me in making logical and salient scholastic choices. He was interested in the end results, not the minutia of the current battle. So that left ME floundering in uncharted waters trying to please the male family elders, my teachers and myself while simultaneously plotting and planning my "supposedly" bright destiny. It would have been great if my father had sat down with me at least once and gave me a bona fide plan of action, a list of appropriate high school classes to take, a list of colleges to explore, a list of offered Stanley Kaplan prep courses, a list of SAT tutors to choose from, a list of eventual engineering or medical schools to apply to, etc. And he easily could have. He was a college professor, working on a mechanical engineering master's degree for God's sake! But no, he did the ostrich thing whenever details of my future life came up in conversation. He only surfaced to check and see if I was there yet and hollered at me if I wasn't. He wanted ME to succeed but HE didn't want to fail. Contrast that to my children's lives. My wife is fond of reminding me that I was frequently "up in their business" when it came to their high school and collegiate endeavors. I WILLINGLY stuck my neck out. I helped them select "correct" high school courses, colleges, etc. I drove them each, hundreds of miles, to visit multiple campuses because it was the right thing to do. I was a hands-on dad and am unashamed of it. For instance, I know that ACTs are easier than SATs, and still remember the admit rates for many top universities! I expected positive results and somehow my kids delivered. I even paid for ALL their schooling. Winning! My mother often mentions to me how proud my father is of my distinguished dental career and accomplishments in life. Really? Great, just great although I hope he smugly doesn't take too much credit for it. I did most of it by myself, except for the tuition paying part. I thank him for that, however. It left me debt free to start my adult life and THAT I continually treasure, as do my children, and their lack of college loans as well. Nevertheless, I never appreciated all the incessant negativity and abusive mental bullshit that I received as an adolescent because the ends don't always justify the means. What if I had turned out to be less than an engineer or doctor? What then: a lifetime of sarcastic, ironic criticisms, innuendos, ridicule and should-have-beens from "loved" ones? Would I still be loved, by anyone? Hello? All I can NOW say is that I most likely got very lucky with my youthful decisions and not only had the willpower and *chutzpah* to follow through with them but frequently eschewed many fun, but "wrong" directions and choices in life, to stay on track. Perhaps my psychologically heavy handed home life had influenced me after all? Anyway, eighth grade was just around the corner; I would be there, fighting with the courses, my old man and my perfectionist self, as usual. But I knew I would make it. I had to; my future was impatiently waiting for me.

43

Uncomfortably Dumb

My insincere apologies to the seminal band Pink Floyd for usurping the title of one of their mega hit songs, garbling it, and using it for my own purposes. Unfortunately, although my seventh-grade odyssey was slowly winding down, I still felt wound up inside. Unlike elementary school, junior high resembled a continuous eight period HIIT (high intensity interval training) class; specified intervals of calm punctuated by sudden outbursts of activity, as classrooms regurgitated wild-eyed students into the hallways for the four-minute dash between periods. None of us *schmucks* knew about homeschooling back in those dark days. Too bad. Maybe an alternative would have been nice to consider? Anyhow, my overall grades were mediocre by my lofty standards and extremely low by my father's educational yardstick. Although pulling a combined low A average, I sensed that I could do more, be more, excel more, but acutely perceived that I was not getting any real traction to "get going." I felt stymied by school, and life in general. My parents' expectations of me were through the roof yet their guidance of an introspective, inquisitive, funny, and nervous young son was next to nil. There was pressure at home, pressure and prejudice at school, and my own internal pressure of succeeding scholastically and athletically. Whether or not based in reality, feeling dumb merely compounded my already elevated levels of academic discomfort and domestic misery. I did have some success musically, artistically (not autistically), and naturalistically, and continued to prosper in science. So, maybe things weren't so dire after all. My tennis acumen and skills were picking up, with a serve and forehand that improved yearly. And my close friends were the same lot of crazy, comedic, misfits, and I was grateful for them. Perhaps a lot of adolescents experienced my sense of alienation, anxiety and feelings of ineptitude while surrounded by peers that were apparently "killing it." To top it off, the previous joyrides that I had experienced on Bus 57 going up and down Pell Hill became boring. What the hell? Maybe it was just me, but I doubt it. Hopefully, the upcoming eighth grade would be a welcome change and not a continuation of the dogmatic drivel that dogged me all year long. Someone, anyone, please throw me a bone!

Take a break!

EIGHTH GRADE

44

Starting Anew

Okay, let's be honest. I really wasn't as prepared for seventh grade as I imagined I should have been. I had pencils, pens and notebooks aplenty and still struggled. I memorized my class schedule and locker combination numbers and still struggled. I hit puberty on a daily basis and still struggled, well, with the ladies that is. Seventh grade had been mentally and psychologically challenging for me and I just didn't live up to my own or my folks' expectations. I carried an A minus average, was in a few afterschool activities, played piano, violin, tennis, and ping pong, and managed to squeeze in some entomological and naturalistic diversions as well. However, I often felt defeated, deflated and demoralized. But why? Was it hormonal? Was it the insanity of the bustling junior high experience, or was it the constant drumbeat of never satisfied parental units that made me feel a failure? Perhaps it was comparing myself to other students that were only now blossoming as intelligent human beings and future competitors? I don't know. Perchance it was all of the above? I thought I was special; I wasn't. I would be starting eighth grade soon and things had to get better; they didn't.

45

Silly Putty and PEZ

Silly Putty: A Crayola made, non toxic, dilatant-flowing, viscoelastic, silicone based polymer that can be stretched thin yet quickly snapped in half. It is sticky but supple, a flesh-hued, putty-like substance that was really good at picking up the old, ink-based colored funnies in newspapers. PEZ: An initially Austrian made, non toxic, hard peppermint candy promoted for smoking cessation that became a huge international hit with the advent of character-stylized twelve slot cartridges, now made in Connecticut, with many different flavors and even collectible plastic dispensers available, with a resultant loyal following. And there you have it. What more can I say? Both were a twelve-year-old's delight. And both were less boring than the Slinky!

46

The "Lost" Summers

No, this is not a vignette for readers to feel sorry for me, and yet, it emphasizes the plight of an adolescent boy missing his father during the summers of '71, '72, and '73. No, I didn't go away to any fancy-shmancy summer camp; HE'S the one that went away, to summer school. Yes, summer school! But first let's back up a bit. Why did pop have to go in the first place? Well, a B.S. only got him as far as an associate professorship. He was basically "forced" to go earn a master's degree, if he had any allusions of being promoted to full professor and attaining a commensurate pay grade. It was called professional improvement by the college higher-ups and lots of his colleagues did it, and, summers were the only times available for such educational endeavors. Rochester Institute of Technology offered a three-summer, intense, master's program in mechanical engineering to qualified professors around the state. So he left, and I stayed to become the man of the house. Not! I forgot about the browbeating, insulting and workaholic Estonian grandfather that would be left behind to boss us three remaining peasants around. Oh, no. And whom would I play tennis with, go fishing with, and shoot guns with? Well, there was always the village pool, and my old entomological mentor Dr. R. to commiserate with. Plus I could play with my sister if I really had to. And I had my trusty Schwinn, so maybe things wouldn't be so dire after all. The summer of 1971, after the completion of elementary schooling, was relatively uneventful unless you figured in the unexpected great flood that devastated our town's downtown area, and the new village septic system that devastated all the streets anew. The Vietnam War was still raging, and my grandpa Pete was still raging at me for not measuring up to HIS standards of manhood. At eleven years old I was caught between being a kid and an adult, with no father at home to help guide me. Mom did her best to help me escape her tyrannical father-in-law, to have some fun in the sun, and not be constantly coerced into participating in the never-ending hard labor seemingly planned for me on a daily basis. I did invariably help out in the garden, and boringly "assisted" my boorish grandpa while HE fixed things around the house. I would frequently run off to the college and hit tennis balls against the large concrete wall that was specifically built for that purpose. None of my peers played; I was on my own. I remember slamming the white balls for practice purposes and out of frustration. On really hot days I would run to the village outdoor pool for an afternoon's swim with some pals of mine. It was free admittance; all you needed was a towel, flip flops and a bathing suit. I knew how to swim well after a few previous summers of swimming lessons in the cold, frosty pool on cool mornings that were common for our area at the time. There was no global warming in the '70s. But to ride my bike, I had to literally carry it over the mounds of dirt and excavated asphalt on my dug up street to get to another road to ride on. The long-awaited sewage project was taking a long time to complete and my patience was wearing thin. And remember, Schwinn cycles of yesteryear were heavy, bulky and not easy to lift. I managed, though. Although I talked to my old man by phone a few times and he managed to come home for a few weekends, the thing I looked forward to the most was our ritualistic two-week excursion to Hammonasset Beach State Park in Connecticut, for our annual ocean holiday camping trip. Pop would be home in late August and our family foursome would be whole again, at the beach, and without that garrulous grandfather of mine. It's funny how much I missed my father and willingly dismissed the pressure and guilt he placed on me during the school year, always sarcastically reminding me of my inadequacies as an athlete and scholar. I usually had my fill of him by every school's end; however, this time he was gone just as I was

done. The following summer, the summer of '72 and after
seventh grade, was a welcome mental respite for me. I had
done rather poorly scholastically, by both my family and
my high standards, and needed to recompose myself. It
was almost a relief to have my scolding and annoyed father
leave again. He thought I should have done much, much
better academically but I foundered instead. My excuses
were feeble and I felt a festering failure. As I slowly
ruminated on seventh grade and sorted things out, I
realized that some things in my summer vacation life were
still a constant: the Vietnam War had no end in sight,
Grandpa Pete continued to be a belligerent bully, my mom
was trying to keep it together as a single parent once more,
and my younger sister was growing up. However, this time
I was determined to stop running away so much and be
more responsible to those around me. Perhaps my
haranguing grandpa had me pegged correctly all along.
Maybe I was a *putz* after all, with just enough brains and
guile to fool people into thinking I was smart; a smart
aleck, yes, but perhaps a *putz* nonetheless. So I changed
things up. One warm day, instead of hunting for jumping
spiders or tiger swallowtail butterflies, I announced that I
was going to repaint the metal railings on our back porch.
Rust spots had crept onto the steel surfaces and a coat of
black paint was badly needed. Grandpa Pete was shocked

at my audacity to do some work but then quietly questioned my skills at painting and reminded me that my perfectionist father would accept nothing short of a professional job. NO pressure there! But I got 'er done. No spills, no messes, and no black paint were found on the porch floor or nearby flowers. Mom was amazed, Grandpa Pete actually smirked. My old man would be pleased. All those winter hours spent gluing miniature models together and shooting toy guns at my plastic soldiers had sharpened my manual dexterity. Not to mention all the times I shot a real weapon, while carefully aiming at hapless woodchucks. One project was done with a few more on my docket. However, first I uncharacteristically asserted myself and made deals with the two adults in my house. I traded work for time off and began to engage my sister as a playmate and confidante. Besides going to the nearby brook to catch my fill of salamanders and visiting my old mentor Dr. R., I started a kickball league using our hilly backyard as the playing field. OK, it was a small league, actually just my sister and me! But it was great sport making up a multitude of teams on paper, giving them funny names and then "playing" for the teams. We took turns between innings rolling the ball to one another, kicking it, and playing all the positions as necessary. The steep hill was an effective backstop and served as extra players to help the defense. We kept score and primitive statistics, and I backed off as necessary to keep things fair athletically. I have to admit that we indeed had fun. Our injured dead-end street was mended after the previous summer's septic installation project and sis and I would ride our bikes on it while I kept an eye on her. I was fast becoming the nauseatingly protective older brother that's a hackneyed cliché in society. I even held her hand and took her swimming with me to give mom a break, so she could wash, iron, clean, sew, plant, cook, till, and weed in peace and maybe catch her breath for a short while. Ha, ha. Before starting on a difficult building affair with my grandpa, I vowed to mow the lawn all summer, and did just that. Was I truly sincere in my efforts at workmanship or just a showoff, flaunting my "newfound" responsible and facile attitude for self-aggrandizement? Maybe both? Regardless, I rolled up my sleeves, so to speak, and earnestly began constructing an addition to our existing wooden garden shed with my grandfather, who was eager to teach me the principles of building. Of course, it was my civil engineer father that was truly the builder in the family; Grandpa Pete mistakenly thought that he had that same knowhow as well. He was only partially correct, however. Although vitally instrumental in the fabrication of our own home, it was my dad's architectural and engineering skills that got the job done right. Grandpa Pete had basically been the brawn of the operation. Anyway, we laid blocks, mixed concrete, put up two by fours, hammered home the shingles and completed the small side wing to our shed in no time. I recall that my pop was duly impressed by it; only later did my grandfather's shoddy engineering skills, sloppy work and inattention to detail rear its head. Pop had to correct the deficiencies himself but praised me for at least involving myself so diligently in the project to begin with. I was growing up, I think. The summer was waning, my dad would be home soon, my mom was packing for our beach holiday, my grandfather took his foot off my throat, and I was pleased with my summer's adventures and many accomplishments. Eighth grade would be starting after our August, oceanic, vacation, and I would be darn ready. Hopefully, that grade would be kinder to me than seventh had been. It wasn't. Anyhow, as I sat "relaxing" on the same Connecticut seashore contemplating my future I realized that I was not ready for yet another bout of a misplaced father, for he would be missing again the following year while finally completing his studies. Somehow, we all muddled through those three long summers, but I can't help but ponder on the deficit of a parent, especially one that was simultaneously a bane and someone to emulate to a reflective young man.

47

Second Helping

I found myself sitting in the same classroom as last year, in the very same front row seat, in the same dark and dreary bus garage building. Help!!?? It was another academic year and another quarter of mandatory, male only, Agriculture class. It would be a second helping of the meaty course I took as a seventh-grader. But wait, what did I have to worry about? I had killed Agriculture 101; perhaps this iteration would be similar? It was, thank goodness. The usual noisy blockheads were parked in the back rows while we "studious" students were in the head positions, close to the blackboard and clutching the valuable textbooks that Mr. F. had just distributed. Without that voluminous volume on all things agriculturally inclined, I would have been sunk. Of course you had to read it, which I religiously did, just like I did last year's book. I was all set. However, the topics covered in eighth grade were difficult to comprehend at times and taught with a more in-depth approach. I won't bore you with the details but suffice it to say that I ended up scoring near the top of the class, learning about such things as grains, various bovine and pork feeds, animal husbandry, artificial insemination, farming practices, how to treat udder rashes, soil conservation, and advanced gardening principles. Wowsers! After that course I was ready to jump on a John Deere tractor, plow a few fields, slop some hogs, and grab some cow teats! But no, I couldn't; I didn't have an official John Deere cap to wear, darn it. And I was so close, too. The quarter ended, I got my A and the backrow bunch of incessant, know-it-all hecklers, got their deserved C's. But, hey, they were going to inherit their daddy's farms, so, all was *kosher* in my bucolic, cattle-infested, milk producing, hayseed bred, town.

48

Still Flailing in Math!

Unfortunately, that title is spelled correctly. I was passing with a high B average, however, by MY standards, was flailing in a class that I should have been acing. What the hell was going on? I was distraught, my mother was clueless as to my numerical misfortune, and my father had already gone ballistic, calling me every name in the book, in the Estonian language that is. Still, it stung me deeply. Why was his only son a brain-dead *putz* when it came to mathematics? Was it puberty? Was the lummox of a teacher partly to blame? There were no easy answers but homework time for me turned into frequent shouting matches with my dad because I did not comprehend the "simple" material in that dang eighth grade arithmetic book. Well, actually, HE did all the hollering, and I didn't say much at all. Firstly, I was stuck in the perceived dumbbell math section while most of my smarty-pants friends were already taking algebra. Secondly, THIS dumbbell was not understanding the dumbbell math! It seemed a double whammy for me. So, how did this scholastic tragedy come to pass, and when would it end? Mr. Foke, the nickname most kids called him by, was the eighth-grade regular math teacher, having graduated from a nearby state university. He basically graduated with a degree in basketball, although his diploma said liberal arts; he was also armed with a teacher's certificate as well. Now you know where his head was really at: at the rim, and not in education. At six foot, six inches tall, he was a *loco* boy (his folks ran two markets in town) and had been a former standout hoop star at my high school. He further developed his ball skills in college and now, voila, he was "teaching" me math while doubling as the assistant varsity basketball coach. He was heir apparent to the high school head coach, who also doubled as the trigonometry/math twelve teacher. I would have Mr. O. as a math instructor in subsequent years. The eighth-grade math had started auspiciously enough but degenerated rather quickly. There was no alphabetical seating in that class and I managed to snag a seat in the front, right next to G.B., who seemed to sit in the right front corner of every class that I had with him. He always had his right side pressed against the wall and twisted his neck and head to the left. Maybe he was hard of hearing out of his right ear and no one knew it. I was hard of learning, at least in math, and lots of people knew it, darn it. Anyhow, I could now see the blackboard with or without my glasses on and would be ready to learn, unlike my arithmetic debacle the previous year. I was determined to double down and "understand" eighth grade math! After we quieted down that first day, Mr. Foke stood up and began to slowly enunciate the plan for the school year. Holy crap, I almost fell asleep. Here was a tall giant of a man, with a baritone voice, speaking as if someone had dropped a Quaalude into his afternoon cup of coffee. He looked stiff, bored and comatose. He was a mope, maybe also a dope, but at least a mope, for sure. Although an athletic specimen, and married to his *hot*, high school sweetheart, who was my former summer swimming instructress and sister of my current gym teacher, he looked unhappy. Perhaps he also hated math, the low salary or teaching us imbeciles? He was a "local," married to a "local," and teaching at his old alma mater. Maybe that was the problem. Nevertheless, as the year progressed I struggled. I understood my other subjects just fine but could not get over the hump in his course. I felt that HE didn't want to be in his own classroom and neither did I. It was a mutual uneasy feeling. Finally, my father stepped in, much to my dismay and consternation. He took it upon himself to give me "math homework" on many Sunday afternoons that HE thought I should learn. Most of the problems were algebraic in nature and didn't really jibe with my current textbook questions but I was coerced into participating in those belittling sessions, if only to prove to my old man that I was not as boneheaded as he thought I was. Of course, if I didn't instantly understand something pop would explode and try to "teach" me math, the hard way, his way. Lots of swearing and name calling was the fare on those select horrible Sunday afternoons. As a civil engineering professor, my father had to dumb down his gray matter and gave me "easy" questions and could not understand why his son was so stupid. I believe my younger sister witnessed our kitchen table learnin' hijinks and saw to it that it would not happen to her. She ended up being much "smarter" than me and *crushed* ALL of her subjects, ALL of the time, and throughout her entire schooling tenure. What a smart lass! Nonetheless, all that miserable mathematical "home schooling" slowly paid off for me. Whether I finally understood some concepts, studied harder, or now always had math on the brain, I started to perk up in Mr. Foke's class. My GPA rose and by the end of the year I actually comprehended a thing or two and even received a few top test scores as well. Pop was shocked, I was shocked, however Mr. Foke didn't seem to notice. He was busy preparing himself to take over the varsity head basketball coaching position, which he did, in 1975. But for now, I despised math less and less and thought I would be ready for algebra, the following year, and I was. Ninth-grade algebra saved me from my old man's math wrath; I actually enjoyed the enthusiastic teacher and killed it, as a future story will elucidate. I finished the eighth-grade math course with a low A average and was grateful that I left that class largely mentally unscathed, no thanks to that gargantuan, mopey, hoopster.

49

Conjugate This....

It was not called eighth grade English or English 8. No folks, it was called Grammar, as if to further drive that knife into our backs and expose our blatant incompetence as young scribes of the English language. The course title conjured up thoughts of seriousness and gravitas. As much as I needed help in my primitive endeavors at proper sentence structure when composing a literary piece, I was still fearful of what lay in store. Perhaps it was merely misplaced anxiety and irrational thoughts on my part. Or maybe what I had heard from many upperclassmen was indeed true: Grammar was a tough-ass course taught by a likewise instructor. Nevertheless, we needed this class to learn how to write, period! I guessed it would help me as I solemnly took a front row seat in the middle of the pew, in a class that resembled a pious and reverent church congregation. Most pupils struggled mightily to coherently and correctly put words together, but this particular course promised to straighten us out, and boy did it ever. Mr. G. taught basic Grammar and took no prisoners. A middle-aged, mustachioed, stout man with a flat-top crew cut and sideburns, he looked like an English teacher, right down to his Mr. Roger's sweaters and polished black shoes. He was at once intimidating and friendly on that first day. But his phony friendliness ended up giving way to profound pronouncements on the rigors of constructing words into meaningful paragraphs that made grammatical sense. Whew. He HAD to be tough, however. Grammar is the backbone of any language and I believe that deep down even the lazy and mediocre students realized that, and gave Mr. G. quarter, and a driblet of respect, sometimes while not understanding a lick of what he was talking about. Nonetheless, the class chugged ahead, with adverbs, adjectives, nouns, pronouns, and verbs up the wazoo. Plus, we had daily ten-word spelling tests with the words given to us the day before, to memorize. After the quizzes, we were implored to exchange our answer sheets with a neighbor and then correct each other's papers before passing them forward to be collected by the teacher. Stress, anxiety and a constant feeling of resentment was palpable among the home crowd as the year progressed. "Conjugate this, conjugate that," were the mantras spewed forth by the unflappable Mr. G. And although he never took delight in a floundering student, he frequently expressed exasperation at our recurring idiocy at something so sublime and easy to understand as grammar. The entire scholastic year was a nail-biting experience for me. The concepts were rough,

Mr. G. was tough, but I persevered as best as I could, learning that soporific and torpid material. Surprisingly, I was flirting with a low A average by the end of the school term. I made it, passed the final exam and breathed a huge sigh of relief on finishing with a grade in the low '90s. Did I now know how to write and how to spell? Maybe, but, in reality, it made me more careful and aware, paying attention to tenses and thought progression, and not glibly and haphazardly putting pen to paper when "trying" to write. Thank you, Mr. G., for a job well done, I think.

50

The Silver Cap

School had already started, and NOW mom wanted my teeth straightened? We had a whole previous summer to do it in! My dad had been away for most of it at RIT, working on his master's degree; I had been doing "nothing," according to my workaholic live-in grandfather, but now that I was knee deep in scholastic shit she went ahead and made me an appointment to see elderly and ill-mannered Dr. Smithe, the only non alcoholic, non drug abuser, non inept dentist in town. The one we had been going to for a few years now. He was the snobbish, lanky, Ivy League (Penn Dental School) educated oldster that practiced "old-fashioned" dentistry on mostly hapless hucksters in our hayseed haven. Hey, he got paid once in a while, so what was he constantly carping about? Anyway, the date was set and I dutifully showed up on time after school at his Main Street residence. I had walked there alone; my younger sister had taken the bus home. Dr. Smithe called my name and I entered his inner lair, the dark and spooky operatory with the gadgets and implements of his trade squeezed into a tiny cubicle. We were all alone; he did not utilize a dental assistant. While craning over me, he adjusted the overhead lamp to focus on my mouth, but the intense beam of light blinded me anyway. "Your mother told me I had to straighten you out," he bellowed sarcastically. I just sat there, glued to the electric chair, unmoving, with my mouth wide open. He looked, he prodded, he grunted and farted. Then he used a small mouth mirror to examine my teeth in detail, one by one. Suddenly, he stepped back, doused the interrogation lamp and told me what was going to happen. Because my parents were too cheap, or ill informed, they had sought the counsel of Dr. Smithe, instead of the orthodontist in the city nineteen miles away. The diagnosis from the orthodontist would have probably been multiple extractions followed by a few years of wearing metal braces, and with a hefty price tag to match. By contrast, Dr. Smithe promised to extract only one upper left tooth and then slide a stainless steel cap onto my left lateral incisor, to bump it over my lower teeth. He further added that my lowers were straight enough and did not need any intervention. My mother read the note he sent home with me and she and my dad agreed to let him have a go at me. Now, I had been to him many times for checkups and small, simple, amalgam fillings, which he always accomplished without using any Novacaine. However, I assumed that this time would be different. How was he

going to yank a tooth from my head without getting me
numb first? Holy moly! I began to get extremely worried
and my fingernails took a beating. Mom gave me twenty-
five bucks that Tuesday morning, which I stuck deep into
my front pants pocket, before leaving for school with my
sister. It was D-day for me, right after school dismissal. I
wasn't in a "funny" mood that morning as the clocks in
every classroom ticked me off by somehow speeding up.
The rest of the afternoon was a blur before I regained
consciousness, and then found myself once again on Dr.
Smithe's "hot seat," with my cake hole stretched wide open.
My heart was racing, and I was sweating profusely.
Goddammit, I was nervous! Old Doc Smithe looked at the
wretched patient below him and chuckled loudly as he
readied a syringe of anesthetic. Thank goodness. He
grabbed my head with his left arm in a modified choke
hold and stuck me with that needle. I didn't move a
muscle. After a few minutes, my cheekbone and upper
teeth fell asleep on the left side of my face. Once more he
tackled my head and deftly extracted my left first premolar
tooth. There was almost no bleeding and I had felt
nothing. Then he quickly mixed up some cement, applied
it to the inside of a silvery cap that he had premeasured,
and glued it over the incisor, as promised. He asked how I
felt, but I couldn't answer with all that gauze in my mouth.

And then he summarily dismissed me to his receptionist, who dutifully collected the money from me, as prearranged with mom. I left the office and quickly walked home, still numb and with cotton protruding from my pie hole. I took back streets so as not to run into anyone I knew; it would have been embarrassing to do so. Lo and behold, his minimalist dentistry started to work. Although my upper bite shifted slightly to the left, with that shiny front tooth acting as an anti chick magnet, my top teeth got their act together and started to line up beautifully. Of course, I had to wear that darn, unsightly crown for six months. At least others in my class, including lots of girls, were already wired up with braces so a little glint out of my mouth was nothing compared to their shimmering dental woes. Months later, as Doc Smithe removed that gleaming metallic glob off my tooth, he muttered some clearly understandable swear words under his breath. It turned out that the cement had washed out from inside the cap and my lateral incisor had become irreversibly mottled with unsightly brown splotches on it. The enamel had been ruined. He didn't say a word as I dejectedly left his office with my mother. Hey, my folks had saved a bundle; what were two sacrificial teeth? Well, one had been pulled, the other crippled, that's what! Now fast forward to my time in dental school. During the second semester of my freshman year, Dr. C., my Dental Anatomy professor, grabbed me in the hallway one day and told me to follow him into the third-year operative clinic, where upperclassmen were drilling and filling on live patients. Dr. C. liked me because I was already then exhibiting signs of excellence as a dental student. As I plopped into an examination chair he asked me politely, but point blank, how I could walk around with a deeply stained front incisor in my mouth? I thought about it and recalled that I had managed to successfully finish high school, graduated from pharmacy college, was a dental student, and was engaged to marry hottie blondie (my future wife's nickname in pharmacy college); all attained in spite of a discolored tooth in plain sight. I was about to make my escape when Dr. C. told me that he could quickly and without cost, fix my smile with a porcelain veneer, a piece of properly colored ceramic which would be cemented onto my derelict tooth. At the time, he was at the forefront of veneer research and needed suckers/ volunteers. I fell into his lap and two visits later he gave me my "winsome" grin back. It was 1983 and I was the second person in New York State to have a porcelain veneer installed in my mouth. And it is still there, somewhat worn around the edges and probably in need of cosmetic replacement, but still in place. I recently found that old steel cap of mine in the back of a drawer I seldom use, and the memories flooded back. I held it in my fingers for a few seconds before chucking it into a waste bin. Some remembrances just had to die.

51

The Hard Way

He was our neighbor and a native son. He was an ice cream vendor and a cherry tobacco, pipe-smoking, middle-aged man living with his aged mother in a circa late 1800s, rundown, paint-peeling house. And he was also blind. Bruce H. and his cantankerous, wisp of a mother came with our street when we had our brand new house built next to theirs. There was some initial tension, some swearwords exchanged over property lines, and some animosity on their part because now they lived next to "Russians," whose adult members had wicked Slavic accents. Of course, THEIR hillbilly enunciation of certain words also gave ME pause, making me wince time and again whenever I interacted with them. So we were about even-steven in the linguistics/pronunciation department. Nevertheless, my family and I were gracious, friendly and civil neighbors; we kept our property immaculate and regularly bought ice cream from them. So all was forgiven and both parties settled in for a long, cordial relationship. I mention Bruce because whenever times were tough for me, which was often, I would remember him cutting the grass on his lawn in front of his dilapidated house. He would use a manual sickle bar mower for the flat parts but how he managed to maneuver those rotating, sharpened blades in a straight line, without leaving streaks, was a mystery. However, that feat was nothing compared to what he accomplished next. His meticulous coifing of the sloped sections surrounding his ramshackle domicile was a real eye opener and a testament to the words perseverance and stubbornness. With Rip, his trusty, golden Labrador Seeing Eye dog watching over him, Bruce would squat on his haunches, grab a handful of green shoots with his left hand and then methodically amputate them at ground level with a pair of gardening shears, which he expertly handled with his right hand. He never hurt himself as I watched him carefully traverse the uneven terrain and get the job done. It was painstakingly slow, with much feeling of the grass involved. I would silently look at him, hunched over, and listen to the click-clacking of the scissors as he sought to keep his property looking as best as it could. He was a tough man with a tough personality, sadly saddled with a tough disability. I would often compare his lot in life with my own "privileged" existence and feel ashamed at my lofty thoughts, dreams and alleged shortcomings. He was blind and didn't complain; what was wrong with me? Everything, as he always brought me down to earth and made me "see" the big picture of life, without actually seeing me at all. He inspired me all those years ago and I passed on that subtle wisdom to my own son, who was also born visually impaired. Thanks, Bruce H.

52

Westward Ho!

I'm not sure why my parents picked that warm fall day to make a trip to their former stomping grounds in western New York State. Perhaps it was because of the nice weather, or maybe a long holiday weekend with Monday off? We had made these expeditions before, since I was a tiny lad, but never in the autumn. Whatever, my parents, my younger sister, and Grandpa Pete clambered into our metallic green 1965 Oldsmobile F-85 station wagon and we took off into the afternoon sun. Our first stop would be a large city on the way, where my mom's folks lived. After driving over back roads and through multiple dusty towns (shortcuts?), and with no bathroom or food breaks allowed, our four-hour journey ended on St. Paul Boulevard, at Grandpa Gregory and Grandma Helen's ornate stucco house. They were always happy to see us, with the exception of my father's father, with whom they still had a longstanding family feud. You know, the typical simmering and ongoing grudges that happen in the best of families, especially immigrant ones. Anyway, we had made it, disembarked, peed, and sat down to a sumptuous, traditional, Estonian dinner. My mother's younger brother, who lived nearby, also showed up with his wife and two kids in tow. It was a mini family reunion of sorts and everyone pretended to play nice, between shots of genuine Estonian vodka for the grownups and "forbidden" Fanta orange soda for us youngsters, while feasting on mounds of fried potatoes, herring, sausage, and beet salad. We slept overnight in the huge house and departed for our final landing place in the early morn, after a killer breakfast of course. We reached our second and final destination an hour later, and just in time to relieve ourselves, at a former neighbor's home, in our old familiar, multi ethnic *hood*. My parents and I had left that industrialized metropolis, and my city of birth, in '64, but Grandpa Pete remained behind, eventually selling the family house, hopping across the state, and moving in with us in 1967. He had driven solo to his old haunts numerous times over the ensuing years to tie up loose ends and visit old friends. I, on the other hand, had not been back since '67, and relished checking out my old street and maybe meeting up with some former acquaintances of mine. I was stoked and ready to meet and greet. However, we all nearly cried as we slowly drove by our occupied old abode and reminisced about the past. It was tearfully sad to see it and not turn into its driveway as a homecoming. Alas, dad steered the car into a one-time neighbor's yard and that's where we refreshed ourselves. The friendly Polish folks that took us in knew in advance that we were coming and fed and watered us. This was also the home of my infamous preschool pal, Steve W., the stout and loud young lad who practically lived at my nearby dwelling back in the day. He would boldly march over unannounced, play with my outdoor and indoor toys with or without me, eat my leftover vittles during lunch and then say that I was the best skinny friend he ever had. I was just glad for some company and, although sickly and emaciated in those days, I looked forward to his visits. Suddenly he appeared before me and we sized each other up. We were now both twelve and hadn't interacted in years. However, the former concentration-camp-looking-boy (me) had grown up into a wiry, athletic, and somewhat articulate young man. Steve W., on the other hand, was a head shorter than me, thin, with long, stringy, mussed up hair and appeared quite knackered for his age. I seemed to have a newfound poise about me, and I confidently chatted up his very pretty older sisters as my dad uncharacteristically bragged about me. Steve W. just cowered and kept his eyes on the floor, as if shamed by my presence. Was he ill? Was school too much for him? Had living the city life beaten him up while his alcoholic father simultaneously beat him down into "submission?" What happened to the always hungry little bulldog that I had grown up with? I never got any answers as we went outside together to round up some old pals. But none were around that day and cell phones weren't invented yet to text them about our presence. The afternoon lolled by with idle and useless chatter from all parties present and then, after quickly loading up on authentic Estonian victuals at the ethnic Broadway Market, we left for home by evening. Yes, we drove for six straight hours in the darkness with no stoppages for food or drink. That's how my family functioned back then: no frills, no stops and no whining. I know my folks were allergic to rest areas, restaurants and strange fodder, but I really had to go to the bathroom. Pop did relent when the begging in the car got too great and he also begrudgingly appreciated some snacks that my mom had surreptitiously squirreled away just in case of trouble. So things weren't as bad as I thought they would be. But during that long trip home, with my sister slouched against me and Grandpa Pete snoring at the other end of the second-row car seat, I couldn't help but mentally rehash that brief interlude that I had with Steve W. He seemed to have capitulated from life at a very young age. Was it the hectic lifestyle, the smog, the city schools, a possible shitty home life surrounded by a decaying metropolis that was doing him in? Perhaps? By contrast, did moving to the country refresh and reinvigorate my body and spirit? Most likely, but I had no easy answers as I fell asleep, gratefully acknowledging my parents' move to greener pastures (literally) and appreciating my adoptive village, bigots and all. I would not see Steve W. ever again, even when my own family and I made that same western trek once more in 1999, this time to attend the funeral of my deceased Grandpa Pete.

53

Explosive Science

I loved science, right? That's what I told myself and others on a daily basis it seemed. Was it all hyperbole and saying the right things to the right people to peacefully keep "them" off my back? Perhaps. But wait, I WAS good in a few scientific endeavors, such as catching, studying and learning about most four-legged, creepy crawly life forms, as well as insects and spiders. So maybe I was a gifted naturalist after all but, as I quickly found out, not really a whiz at the basic science courses. I had garnered a low A in last year's Life Science class with old Mr. N., and tepidly looked forward to Physical Science with old Mr. R., the husband of my future, beloved, English and Creative Writing teacher. Physical Science seeks to explore four general areas: physics, chemistry, earth science and astronomy. Our eighth-grade course was limited to physics and chemistry instruction, with earth science relegated to ninth grade and chemistry re-taught in 11th grade, and physics in 12th. We did not study astronomy per se. Mr. R., our skipper, would best be described as a bespectacled, slender, thin-haired and quiet-spoken *nebbish*. The kind of man that looked like a droll and boring science teacher; his visage did not disappoint that image. However, what started out as a rather dull discourse on physical science ended up with a weekly bang, literally! During the physics montage, Monday through Thursday was spent teaching us dumbbells the fundamentals of mass, energy, Newtonian concepts, matter, space and time, velocity and momentum. Fridays were reserved for lab experiments that Mr. R. performed as if a magician, standing behind a granite-covered lab counter at the front of the class. He would don safety goggles and got right to it, all the while jabbering about what he was doing. And without fail, every stinking experiment either produced an unpleasant odor or blew up in his face, oftentimes hurting him in the process. We didn't know whether to laugh or cry. He tried so hard, yet even the tamest of liquids, solids and gases seemingly had it out for him and apparently sought some sort of vindictive revenge. That's what it looked like, anyway. Burned thumbs and ties, ruined suit jackets, singed hair, melted safety glasses and holes in his shirt from spilled sulfuric acid were the norm for him on those freaky Fridays. Yet, despite the frequently disastrous and calamitous outcomes, he started to endear himself to us in a weird sort of way. I was starting to like that guy. At least we learned NOT to combine baking soda with vinegar – VOLCANO, or drop tiny pellets of sodium metal into cold water   KABOOM! And it was much the same when we began studying chemistry, well, perhaps a bit worse. On Fridays it got to the point where the front row students would back up their desks a few feet, all the while smiling and wide-eyed, just itching for the poppycock to begin. I guess we did learn something about chemical equations, atoms, bonding, and the composition of molecular structures. And then we had those end-of-the-week "fireworks" to look forward to. Kind of like a "reward" for four days of hard work. His tests were on the difficult side and he had a strange way of grading them. They were mostly one-page multiple choice affairs. After the exam he would gather the thirty or so answer papers, collate them, and place his master key on top. Then he would whip out his long, sharpened awl and, with grunts and guffaws, push the pointy tool through the correct answers on his copy and through the rest of our papers. It took him one minute, max, to accomplish that feat as we looked on in amazement. Then he would scan each individual student answer sheet and deduct points where the circled response and awl hole did not meet. After five more minutes, he would be finished and passed the exams back to us for review. After the review he would collect them again to register the grades in his gradebook. It was a very efficient and quick way to mark papers, I must say. I pulled a high

B-plus average in that class and was glad when it was over. Mr. R. had turned out to be a rogue and mad scientist at heart, disguised as a mild mannered high school *lehrer*. I genuinely liked that guy but that was quite enough explosive science for me!

54

Stringing Us Along

E.G., F. and I continued to *play* second violin with the varsity orchestra into eighth grade, under the tutelage and guidance of our feckless teacher/conductor, the inscrutable Mr. Daye. And let me tell you folks, he was a panic; an out and out panic! Many was the time when I would see him frantically running down the hallway, clutching his left breast shirt pocket with his right hand so his pens and cigarette pack wouldn't fall out, while angrily shouting the word "walk" at the top of his lungs at students that he deemed were striding too briskly. He was always in a hurry, always late for lessons and orchestra rehearsals, and endlessly on the phone in his music room. Who was he talking to? His broker, his bookie, his paramour? He looked like a cross between Allan Stewart Konigsberg (aka Woody Allen) and Don Knotts, with bushy hair, big eyes, glasses, and a frail physique. Though not an outwardly athletic type, he managed to constantly be in motion, and I noticed that. He had been a mainstay at our high school for decades, and we novice violinists were just the next jerks in the pipeline of his orchestral ministrations and recalcitrant lessons. We knew his heart wasn't into it anymore, but we went along with the gag and performed as best as we could, to at least keep his spirits up because we liked him. By day he was a high school music instructor; by night, a performer/player himself. He once told me that he played the cello professionally for the Binghamton Philharmonic Orchestra with a stand-mate called Miss Knight. It was day and night with him, as we both laughed at his joke. He had numerous children by the same wife, all of whom were exceedingly musically talented on stringed instruments. During my high school tenure, one of his daughters played an excellent viola while his virtuoso, look-a-like son, was first chair cello in our mostly talentless and meager string section. The rest of us *Mozarts* barely passed muster as musicians, including me. Piano was my forte, not the violin, but somehow my chums and I kept at it, with Mr. Daye encouraging us halfheartedly while continually making those blasted and mysterious phone calls on our time. However, during the scheduled school recitals, with parents and school brass in the audience, he was all business and would not pick up his baton until uttering his familiar and reassuring catchphrase to us: "Keep your good eye on the music and your bad eye on me." That statement always cracked me up as I positioned my cocked arm and rosined bow above my violin strings and watched for his command to commence firing. Notwithstanding, during the daily orchestral rehearsals, my friends F., E.G. and I would fool around to our hearts content, even making Mr. Daye chuckle at times. Sure we played the right notes and always on cue, but between stoppages we often went feral, much to the delight of those around us. E.G. ended up abandoning the fiddle but F. and I stuck with it. We sat together at the same second violin stand and it was the beginning of a years-long comedic bromance betwixt us. We would carry that friendship through many self-written humorous stage performances as well as impromptu, daily offerings of unbridled and offbeat levity that was enjoyed by our school peers. By seating us together, Mr. Daye had unknowingly created a concrete bond between F. and me that lasted for more than a decade, before cracking and petering out in pharmacy college during our second year there. Thank you, Mr. Daye, for your acceptance of our impertinence and sophomoric wisecracks all those years ago in junior high, and we weren't even sophomores, yet! Believe me, the *worst* was yet to come.

55

Study Halls

They appeared to be perks of high school, with junior high included. And like in seventh grade, the eighth-grade study halls were run much the same way, with participants delineated by their grade point averages. Firstly, what was a study hall for anyway? Well, it was a break in the action, a free period to study, to plagiarize a library book passage, to doze, or to crib important notes or lab results from a friend prior to the next class. You know, legit school things to do besides your own homework. Secondly, depending on your report card marks, different rooms would be utilized to house the pupils for a short while. If a student had an overall A average from the previous scholastic quarter, then he/she could head to the *unstructured* study hall places, such as the library and high school auditorium seating area, with minimal administrative adult supervision. A hushed tone was generally enforced but whispering and moving about was permitted. The *structured* study hall for junior high was held in the high school auditorium balcony, and strictly patrolled by monitors. If you had less than a ninety average, this was your place, for now. NO talking, NO murmuring under your breathe, NO sleeping, NO nothing. You had to sit there, read and study, a seat apart from the next person. The structured balcony banishment, however, resembled a punishment of sorts, without any initial deleterious behavior noted from anyone! Nevertheless, one could escape to the library if you had a very good reason to go there. All first quarter students were deployed in the balcony section but many, including me, left after those all-important first quarter grades came out, separating the "smart" from the "stupid." However, even an intelligent pupil could be demoted for grossly violating that sacred privilege of exceptionalism bestowed on her/him. You had to know how to duck the ire of the umpires and referees present, in order to get your jollies in. Looking back, I would have taken an extra class in something, or sincerely studied. Instead, I wasted that daily free period quietly fooling around with my other smarty pals and did not accomplish a whole heck of a lot. My folks never questioned the study hall concept and wrongly assumed that I was rigorously and diligently preparing myself academically in that forty-plus-minute junket. Ha, ha. Anyway, much later, in high school proper, I did start to use that time off wisely, if only to do last minute unfinished homework or to cram for an upcoming exam that I didn't adequately prepare for the night before. And by then the rules were relaxed for all 9-12 students, with a senior lounge provided for twelfth graders. Paradoxically, I could have talked and goofed around to my heart's content but really studied instead. However, in junior high, jerks like me and my fellow jesters abused the system; we did everything BUT study. The unstructured study halls remained a mainstay of our comedic horseplay, albeit "on the QT," silently subverting the librarian and all those administration shills that sought to squelch our growing shenanigans. I know, I know, we could be really immature twits at times, as I'm sure most of our female classmates would readily attest to.

56

Smoking in the Boys' Room

Props to Brownsville Station for their 1973 smash hit *Smokin' in the Boy's Room*, an anti-authoritarian rock ballad about getting away with smoking cigarettes in high school restrooms. And I'm sure they meant girls' bathrooms as well, maybe more so. Relatively tame elementary school vices such as eating candy and chewing gum during class time gave way to cigarette smoking and the beginning of dope sampling by eighth grade. Some students picked up the fixation from home, some from being curious, and others from a "typical" adolescent rebellious streak. And I'm not just speaking of the boys; the girls' lavatories also had acrid, white smoke pouring out from under the outer doors at different times of the day, especially early mornings. You had to get your fix in early to be able to put up with the teachers' bullshit, at least until lunchtime when you could secretly take a drag again! Sure, we had buying-age restrictions and school anti drug/tobacco laws back then too, but ingenious pupils managed to circumvent them and continued their "misguided ways." The no nonsense smoking principal, teachers, health instructor, and available high school "cancer stick" cessation literature all did not seem to halt their emerging hardcore habits. But regardless of the pervasive advertisements extolling the seemingly harmless sexiness of lighting up back then, everyone knew of the dangers that tar and nicotine posed. However, as today, tobacco is still around and people are continually getting hooked. And I'm positive that dopey "juvenile delinquents" are still smoking and toking in the boys' room.

57

Dad's Job

I had visited pop's office at the college campus numerous times, gazed at his nameplate affixed to the heavy oak door, sat in his swivel chair, and admired his neatly organized desktop. He even had color photos of my sis and me in the righthand corner, on top of the immaculate and unstained green blotter. His space was open and inviting as opposed to his office mate's, which was on the other side of an opaque glass divider. That half of the office was a disaster, with papers strewn all over, empty Styrofoam coffee cups littering the floor, stains of unknown origin on the adjacent walls, taped up scribbled notes, and gnarled textbooks in every nook and cranny. It was sort of like seeing *The Odd Couple* in real life. Upon entering, an unsuspecting person would obviously surmise that the neat one did no work in a no-show job at best, while the messy one had deep thoughts while rummaging through the deep paper jungle piled high on his desk. The truth was the opposite, of course. I often marveled at the dichotomy of my father's office environment, working together with that caffeinated and slovenly fellow all day long. Also, upon coming home nightly, dad "rewarded" us family members with the gossip, scuttlebutt and "dirty" office politics as a civil engineering professor at that miniscule Ag and Tech. The college grist was juicy, it was salacious, and it was even mediocre. Oftentimes pop would regale us with intriguing stories that made professorial lecturing sound like the most difficult and underhanded job in the world. The back stabbing, innuendos, deceitfulness, and the wanton deplorable attitudes of the custodians up through and including the departmental chairman made one wonder if there was any teaching going on at all, or just daily infighting and bullshitting among the staff members. My subdued family sat riveted around the dinner table and soaked it all in and marveled at how my old man could continually stomach such a horrible place of employment. It seemed that the daily drama and his mental trauma were part of a never ending soap opera. We even had the cast of "villainous characters" memorized, as if we were all part of a melodrama with no finish in sight. Was being a professor that hard? No, it wasn't. Years later, when my mom, the former "doormat housewife," began teaching Spanish and French at the same college, it dawned on me that perhaps my father's former stories might have been slightly exaggerated, or maybe retold from a biased perspective. My mother's effervescent personality and loquacious disposition made her an instant campus favorite among both instructors and students. She brought home no such stories of depraved malfunctioning professors and manufactured collegial strife, and told my dad to lighten up. It turns out that his perfectionism, tidiness and altruistic approach would have resulted in any job being stressful for him. He took too many things to heart and rather than exploding at work, he internalized his perceived slights and took his "work" home with him…. And all those years I thought that teaching was a monstrous undertaking and a super-anxiety-inducing vocation. The joke was on me all along. I have frequently mentioned to my dad that he wouldn't last a minute as a dentist, putting up with the undeserved aggravation saturation and psychologically corrosive stressors that are inherent in the field. He would always laugh heartily and nod in agreement. I think he realized that his former college teaching tales were no match for a demanding and damning profession such as dentistry. But, despite his complaining, my dad lasted as a distinguished and popular professor for over thirty years and he retired happy, as did my mom, after her twenty-five-year stint. Perhaps blowing off steam by complaining on a nightly basis was pop's way of relaxing but it sure did scare me at the time. Contrarily, I made it a point to rarely discuss anything dental to my own children unless it had a humorous tinge to it. Sure, I privately complained to my old lady (hottie blondie), and still do, even though I now drill part time. But now the kids are out of the house, the cats don't care, and my long suffering wife just nods and pretends to understand. I love her.

58

Mispronunciations

I'm sure it happened in lots of families, whether Estonian immigrants or not. However, in my family it occurred often, especially if I wasn't vigilant. Granted, there were times when certain words were spoken that I believed to be "legitimate" because I had been hearing them since my birth. Others, I managed to correct so as not to let my already accent-burdened parents and grandfather perpetuate a mispronunciation. For instance, my grandpa Pete was infatuated with a popular bowler of the '50s that he called *Vereepoppa*. I incorrectly accepted that it was the guy's first name, not his surname. Whenever we caught a PBA match on TV, that name got invariably dropped as the standard to measure all bowlers by. My dad would get annoyed and often compared grandpa's favorite bowling hero to the Harlem Globetrotters, all show and with a fixed outcome. Heated arguments between the two would ensue while I numbly watched strikes and spares on the set. Only much later in life would I realize that Grandpa Pete was referring to Andy Varipapa, a legendary bowler from yesteryear that often had his own self-effacing, promotional TV shorts, emphasizing his prowess on the lanes with trick shots while appealing to Americans to pick up the sport of bowling. Another very prominent television show was the long running (in syndication, too) Lawrence Welk Show, entertaining generations of viewers with wholesome song and dance numbers. As a child I never bothered to look at the opening sequence to read the name of the production. The adults in my family referred to it as 1, 2, 3, and I knew what they meant: it was time to relax and enjoy the accordion music of Myron Floren, the tap dancing of Arthur Duncan, and the vocalizing of the 'Champagne Lady' – Norma Zimmer. Imagine my surprise when I just happened to see the opening title one day, in fine calligraphic script. I was confused; the theme music was the same, the bubbles were the same but where were the numbers 1, 2, 3? Like a duped dimwit, it finally dawned on me that I had been watching a mispronounced presentation. When I confronted my mom, she shrugged and said that they always called it that; it was part of our familiar family vernacular. I protested and immediately announced that just because Mr. Welk began most musical numbers with his German-accented catchphrase, "And-ah-one-ah, and-ah-two-ah, and-ah-three-ah," didn't make it right for us to bastardize the real namesake of his show. No one said a word when I finished complaining; mom and dad still call it that to this day. The last example of wordy misuse involved one of Grandpa Pete's best loved female singers, whom he referred to as *Sahravonn*. I had never heard of her because even though she had been a dazzling jazz star, it was before my time. But that name kept periodically popping up in my household, as a songstress with no equal. And again I wrongly assumed that it was either a first or last name, not a conglomeration of the two. One day in school my pal E.G. serendipitously mentioned that his parents had discarded some old Sarah Vaughan records and asked me if I wanted them. He even showed the albums to me. I jokingly replied, "Why would I want that rubbish?" I hated the caterwauling and off-key wailer Aretha Franklin and humorously stated that Sarah Vaughan was probably in that same category of shrieking cats. We both cracked up hard and I never got the LPs from him. Later that night, I facetiously and laughingly told my grandfather about my near debacle in receiving *tainted* recordings by some black chick named Sarah, or something like that. He excitedly started babbling, "*Sahravonn, Sahravonn*," as I embarrassingly said nothing and sullenly looked down at my feet. He implored me in Estonian if I could still get those vinyl records. Alas, I could not as my friend had given them to someone else. How could I have known that *Sahravonn* and Sarah Vaughan were one and the same? I imagine I could have guessed, if I had really thought about it. However, during that split-second comic moment involving E.G., the correct pronunciation didn't register with me and Grandpa Pete lost out. Too bad for him. Sorry.

59

To Your Health!

It's a fairly common refrain, especially when toasting someone. But for us junior high grunts, it was literally TIME for health, taught by the indefatigable Mrs. R.G. She was the seventh and eighth grade and high school health instructress in our mini, glorified *reform school*. I'm sorry, that came out sounding rather harsh, I'm afraid. Well, I didn't mean it. My academy wasn't really for incorrigibles or chronic truants but a public central school for the local public's youngsters; where public swearing was forbidden, and civil decorum enforced. I swear I only used that quaint word *ain't* on purpose and only on Bus 57, just to alarm and aggravate my little sister who used to sit next to me. But I reckon we backward baboons DID pick up some needed intelligence from our lowly school because it said so on our cardboard quarterly report cards! So all was not wasted inside that smallish, red brick building perched atop that picturesque hilly pasture, where the local hill folk and "others" sent their progeny to become *edumacated*. Unfortunately, health class was not one of those subjects that instilled we student types with loads of knowledge. Grossly outdated, out of touch with the current times, and with a matching old-fashioned textbook, it was old school "unhealthy" hokum at its worst. And just like last year's iteration, this year's rendition of Health was no different. Sure, we learned about dental and personal hygiene, nutrition, the horrors of cigarette and drug addictions, the various stages and role playing in humanoid life, basic contraception methods, etc. But where were the psychological aspects of dating 101? Not to mention the saucy human element with consequently descriptive mating rituals? I knew it was a lot to ask for but still…. Instead, what we got was technical and uninspiring pablum. Although well presented, the material was appallingly retro, harkening back to the 1950's type of stereotypical dogma. I admit that the fleeting discussions on people's naughty bits woke me right up, but other than that it just devolved into futile attempts to instill in us some rudimentary principles about the anthropoid personage without lecturing us on what it is to be truly human. I already knew about the birds and the bees and how the *parts* and *pieces* fit together; I wanted to know the where and when, and with whom, if you know what I mean. I needed some tips, some insider information on the opposite sex, darn it! However, as opposed to spending more time on the sexuality section, we alternatively learned how to pick nits out of hair, how to incorrectly brush our teeth, and how to interpret the now debunked food pyramid. Nevertheless, Mrs. R.G. did the best as she could with an archaic textbook and hopelessly outmoded "conservative" teaching methodologies. We took it all in stride and most of us received A's for our efforts. Was it a worthwhile course? I guess so. I read the text, listened once in a while but left that class still unable to figure girls out. Perhaps that's just how heterosexual thirteen-year-old boys thought back then? Or, did they?

60

Metallurgy 101

I had aced Wood Shop the previous year, so I figured that eighth-grade Metal Shop would be a similar animal, what with the same teacher and in the same location. Okay, we would be working with iron and steel instead of plywood and lumber but the overall concept of using your hands to "make something" was still the prevailing theme. I wasn't worried as I trudged through the deep snow to the separate bus garage building next to our school and stepped into the same, vacuous, room with about thirty other boys. A few of my friends were among them; however most were those unpleasant male peasants that you could tell were just drooling at the prospect of finally doing something "useful" and not learning that silly stuff called art and music. It was only a quarter course and I was thankful; unafraid, but thankful nonetheless. In walked elderly Mr. S., and proceeded to lay a small square of plywood on the cold, concrete floor while gathering us around him like a gaggle of geese. I knew it was going to be some type of demonstration, but of what kind? The yakking and restless rednecks instantly grew silent as Mr. S. whipped out his old-fashioned pocket knife, expertly opened it, and threw it rather nonchalantly at the wood at his feet. The point stuck in beautifully with an audible thud. Then in quick succession he proceeded to demonstrate his favorite pastime as a kid: Mumbley Peg. The object of the game was to toss the knife, point first, into the ground or board by using various hand positions, angles of the body and knife rotations. After many rounds, as determined by the players, whoever got the most "stick-ins" won. Well, Mr. S. never missed as if he still played regularly. Did he though, at his age? Was he in a Mumbley Peg league, or something? One never knew for sure about such *secrets* in our neck of the deep woods, and no one asked him! Anyway, the "dairy dunces" surrounding him were intrigued and were literally jumping up and down at the chance to play. "Not so fast, boys," Mr. S. excitedly said, while pocketing his pocket knife. "First you have to make your OWN knife, before you can throw it. Welcome to Metal Shop," he added. I recoiled in horror at all those statements. Make your own sanctioned weapon, in school? Was this happening in all high schools across the country, I thought? Well, if I could whittle a piece of timber into a table lamp, jigsaw a cutting board, and carve a cheese tray out of mahogany, maybe I could manage a blade? But wait, Mr. S. had another announcement: "All those boys that do not wish to fabricate daggers can make something else, as long as it is metallic in substance." Whew! However, what should I make? We had a few days to think it over because for the first week, while the antsy goobers in the back rows were squirming to get started on their shanks, Mr. S. explained basic metallurgical principles to the class. Rudimentary casting, swaging, forging, and chemical know-how were taught, prior to letting us loose in the shop. To be honest, the nerdy *mensches* like me slunk to the wussy side of the room while the hot shot heroes organically gravitated to the hot, forging area to begin the process of knife-making. I decided to make a tame paperweight. It was relatively easy. First you shaped and carved a piece of wax into a desired figurine, then you invested it in a plaster mold and let it harden before you melted out the contents and injected hot, molten metal inside, using a centrifuge (the Lost Wax Method). Of course, Mr. S. helped me at all the crucial stages involving propane and acetylene torches, and usage of the whirling centrifuge. After my metal object solidified, I broke open the gypsum covering and out fell my miniature anvil-shaped paperweight, an accurate duplicate of my former waxed up model. It's interesting that in a course called Dental Materials Science, during my first year of dental school, we freshmen students also had to handle acetylene torches, wax, plaster, molten gold, Bunsen burners, propane flames, etc. to gain a basic knowledge about dentistry. Nevertheless, after that initial inoculating dose of eighth-grade metal shop, I became a pro among all the elitist, city slicker dental students that didn't know, or want to know, about such "country crap." The spoiled, Long Island born, Jewish American Princesses in my class suffered most of all in that course. They were going to be dentists, not "fuckin' farmers," God forbid. Meanwhile, I became an instant star, knowing that you had to open the acetylene valve before adding oxygen to get that pointy blue flame going (A before O). Dr. B., my dental materials row instructor, was frequently amazed at my bon vivant attitude and skill at manually carving things and all metalwork involved. But then, when I accidentally informed my fellow peers that I was from "Bumfuck," N.Y., the gig was up. Suddenly, my "materials" acumen made sense. Of course I knew what I was doing; I was probably one of those outhouse using, mud-wallowing hicks from an Indian Reservation in upstate New York that killed and ate skunks, routinely fixed John Deere tractors, and made his own beer and mulberry wine. You know what I mean? I laughed at the time but silently thanked old Mr. S. Anyhow, back to eighth grade and my project. I sanded, polished and presented my pitiful paperweight to Mr. S. He gave me a B, and I deserved it. Meantime, those *man-boys* on the other side of the shop were busy forging, hammering, grinding, sharpening, and often sweating to get their full-tang knives to perfection. Mr. S. spent the majority of his valuable time on "that" side of the room, to make sure the *boyz* wouldn't hurt themselves too badly. And all of them received A's for their efforts, and all went on to make custom wooden handles to encase the beautifully polished mini swords in their calloused hands. I was jealous. Now, on to the next phase of learnin': arc welding. I was ambivalent and resigned to my homespun fate; ain't it the truth, though? But the rough and ready passel of *home boyz* could hardly wait for the sparks to fly. What was wrong with "them?" What was wrong with me? We began slowly, by donning dark, welder's face shields and learning how to turn the high voltage welding machines on and off by feel, in separate booths standing in a long row. You couldn't see anything because of the extremely darkened lenses which were necessary for the next step. Mr. S. secured a foot-long, consumable, positive electrode into our gloved right hand and attached the negative electrode to the heavy piece of metal we were "welding," to create an electrical current when they touched each other. The object for us initiates was to create a scar across the surface of the base metal as if we were joining two metallic objects together in real life. The top layer of slag deposit was then hammered off to expose the weld that we had made. An accurate and straight-lined bead got you an A. I came close, but no cigar. Mr. S. had made it sound simple, but it was not. The machines were turned on and as soon as the electrode "stick" in our hand grazed the electrified chunk of metal before us large sparks flew in all directions, scaring the daylights out of me. What the hell was a fine-fingered pianist doing in this den of fiery hell? The damn sparks, the heat, the deafening sound, and episodic bolts of light were downright frightening. However, the intense light generated allowed me to see what I was doing while ensconced behind an awkward mask. I did okay, good for another B. Others, including most of the adolescent bumpkins, did much better than I. Oh well, at least I had sissy music and art to look forward to. However, I had learned a great deal, although maybe not knowledge that was obviously useful at the time. But as we have already elaborated on, both my pharmacy and dental professional learning processes seemed to have borrowed at least a few nuggets from my boyhood roughneck education in that dang bus garage building and the future is when I really shined. Thank you, Mr. S.

61

Alpine English

As previously stated, eighth-grade grammar was a very difficult course to teach and learn. However, it was made doubly rough by the indoor environment as well. What? That's right; those hapless students that sat next to the windows not only got a good dose of fresh air, but snowflakes in their hairdos, too. Let me explain. At the start of the academic year, when we plebes first entered that den of "iniquitous" English, I was somewhat calmed by Mr. G.'s benevolence of allowing the windows in the classroom to be wide open, thereby giving the adjacent students refreshingly blissful breezes on hot autumn days. The rest of us buffoons also benefitted, inhaling the same cool rivulets of circulating air. Our *country* high school did not have central air conditioning, you know. But wait just a cow-milking-minute.... It was now December and the windows were still open, with ferocious, howling winds and snow swirling into the classroom on most days. All students were told by Mr. G. to wear appropriate attire to his class because the windows would stay open, no matter what. Was he a sadist, a cruel taskmaster, or at least an uncaring *putz*? No, he claimed that students were kept

226

awake by a good dose of Nordic weather, especially when verb conjugation was lectured on. Holy frostbite, Batman! I felt bad for those guys and gals next to the windows. What started as THE place to sit in the fall became a nightmarish, wintry hell for them. The water radiators under the windows were running full blast keeping the students' legs warm, but their upper bodies and heads were often freezing. They resembled a toboggan team, all in a row, unmoving, racing down a hill, with ruddy faces and clutches of snow stuck in their hair. It was a comical sight to see. Sweaters and coats were mandatory clothing in his class during the winter months and no one dozed off while contemplating a dangling participle or the proper usage of a pronoun. Thank goodness for the upcoming spring. Mr. G. and I never interacted on a personal level, except for the many times that I correctly answered his tedious classroom queries. So I was surprised and shocked on that nondescript day after his final exam, as I was walking home, when he accosted me while in his car. He rolled down his driver's side window and I literally froze. He smiled broadly and told me that I had received a 92 final grade average in his course and that it was his pleasure to have taught such a conscientious and studious pupil. Really? He wished my parents a good day and said he greatly looked forward to having my younger sister in his class in the near future. I was still frozen in place as I nodded and grunted back at him. He took off and as he did I realized that maybe, just maybe he was okay. Perhaps his tyrannical and dictatorial teaching methods had been necessary evils to pound some English sense into our largely vacant craniums at the time. As I started my homeward trek, still reeling from the sudden congratulations foisted upon me by him, I ruminated that perhaps he wasn't so bad after all? Thanks, Mr. G.

62

The Little Theatre

As already mentioned in this dreary tripe of a book or in my previously published volume of alleged elementary school hijinks, readers will note that my adopted village was devoid of the simple pleasures in life, such as possessing a bowling alley, a decent restaurant, a bar that served alcohol (we were a *dry* town until the very late '70s), a mall, a decent diner, a movie theater, a sex shop, a strip club, etc. The sequestered college kids up on the hill had their own lives and excitements but the locals, dairy farmers and we high school students had zilch. And I mean zilch. Okay, we had a village pool and tennis courts, both of which I lived at, but what about everyone else? Enter the small-seated auditorium at the collegiate Ag and Tech that was magnanimously opened to the public for no-charge, weekly film viewing, year-round; probably to butter up the native rabble to prevent any kind of deleterious townie/techie interactions. The college was not only good for its extensive library, athletic facilities and reefer, that insidiously trickled over to the high school, but now it extolled wholesome entertainment for the entire family. Sure, most villagers partook as cheering spectators at the college wrestling matches and basketball games, however admission-free movies were the bomb! Of course while many of the flicks were G-rated and from the dustbin of history, we relished the chance to sit in a "real" movie house on Sunday afternoons, sans popcorn, and view classics like *Finian's Rainbow, The Apple Dumpling Gang, The King and I, The Bridge on the River Kwai*, etc. Hey, the motion pictures were scot-free as was the heavily chlorinated water squirting out of the drinking fountains in the outside hallways! Of course that auditorium was normally used by the college students for dramatic events and musicals, as well as a showcase for their own films. But for us townsfolk, that tiny, darkened, veloured place represented a haven of photo-play relaxation and was something to look forward to on weekends and was aptly named The Little Theatre.

63

"Say Something Nice?"

That's what it said on the back of his brown, UPS-like, delivery truck, minus the question mark. Are you freakin' kidding me? There wasn't a more oxymoronic statement than that piece of bullshit, boldly emblazoned on that vehicle, for all to read. Here's the back story: As previously mentioned, my father bought most of our household appliances and electronics from this guy. He was a chain-smoking, plain-spoken, in-your-face, tall, native son. Sometimes belligerent and bellicose, yet at times charming and conciliatory, he always "delivered" the goods, and kept his promises. As a smalltime village vendor of appliances, in a main street storefront that was a former butcher's shop, he could not hide or run away at the first sign of trouble but had to "face the music," on a daily basis. Be it a disgruntled buyer, warranty work, faulty new washers, or clothes dryers that didn't dry. He was always on duty; kind of like an emergency room physician for toasters and TVs. Sure, there was another electronics store in town; however P., with his swagger and bombast, had the local market cornered. He often appeared disgruntled, gruff and at wit's end, but most townsfolk put up with him, including us.

My mom, dad and Grandpa Pete treated him and his extended family like family, and his distant Slavic roots further made him palatable. His teacher-wife and kids were well known around town, yet none of his offspring inherited his larger-than-life persona. Thank goodness. One was enough. It was always a *trip* to visit his store, watching him bicker over prices with luckless rubes, or to see him in person making a delivery to our home and purposely chatting up my parents in very broken Russian. With a smile and always a smart-alecky retort, he would easily banter with my folks in his raspy, cigarette and vodka conditioned voice. What a salesman, what a character he was. But wait. What was that? Now he had purchased a "new," brown delivery truck with a daft slogan printed on the back door in huge white letters. It was facetious, it was outrageous, but it made people stop, stare and consider his business. It was smart public relations. P. eventually closed up shop and moved his business across the street to his large home and continued selling and servicing his wares from his back porch and family room. I presume it saved him a lot a headaches and overhead costs, but customers still sought him out for their household gizmos. We would often drive by and there was THE truck, parked in front of his house, and there was P., heatedly arguing with someone on his front

lawn. What a scene, what a nightmare, for the would-be
buyer! P., we loved you.

64

Still Athletically Inclined

No matter what my height-challenged gym teacher Mr. K. inferred, I was a rising jock, but not in the conventional sense of the word. Even in junior high, most of the favored, white, village scions participated in the esteemed team sports of football, baseball, and basketball with fanatical, future, fecund, female mates egging them on from the sideline cheerleading squads. "The handsome sportsman dates the cheerleading hottie" was in vogue at our pastoral high school, but, alas, not for me. No, I was good at solitary sprinting and especially tennis, that namby-pamby sissy sport for the elites, whoever they were. Did we even have any of those in our one-horse and one stoplight town? I had weathered the biased gym periods of seventh grade and received top grades because my visible athleticism could not be squelched or stopped. Though most of the overt prejudices against my family and me were slowly waning, there were leftover pockets of it that I could not readily overcome. A case in point was team athletics. I was never "one of them," a "native son," that with prodding, extra coaching, and nepotism could rise up and perhaps become a D1 college star someday. No, I was a brown-skinned, black-haired, "foreign transplant" from western New York with a funny last name who tried to play nice with the aboriginal *boyz* and locally born gym teachers while desperately keeping my sporty ego intact and forging ahead, against the grain of injustice and perceived racism. But I persevered, darn it. Fortunately for me, my old man was not only a superb multisport athlete but a professor and tennis coach at the dinky junior college in town. He not only taught me the rudiments of ping pong but also the skill set necessary for his true love – tennis. Although as yet not officially on the varsity team, the high school tennis coach was salivating at the prospect of my future membership and told me so in no uncertain terms. He also gave me a varsity sports duffle bag as an obvious bribe for my eventual capitulation to the often undermanned and unpopular team. You know, tennis, the racquet sport that only "rich" people play. Unfortunately, even as a standout player in upcoming years, there were never any hot babes standing around the courts rooting for me and hoping for a hookup. Actually, there was no one standing around for that matter. The redneck ruffians were not fans and didn't care. I had a great smile and an even greater forehand but was not a home-grown, dimwitted footballer. Oh, well. Track was another one of my strong suits, at least in gym class outings. I routinely bested the football running backs and basketball point guards when running short distances, much to the demonstrative displeasure of Mr. K., the Phys Ed teacher, who doubled as the JV basketball, varsity football and track coach. Ninth grade was just around the corner and I would be ready to smack some tennis balls around at the varsity level. My only lament was that tennis and track seasons were both run simultaneously in the spring and I couldn't do both at the same time. I obviously chose tennis and never looked back. Today, I continue to play, in between necessary knee surgeries, that is. Of course, my exploits in sprinting and javelin throwing mirror my tennis prowess, as I have continued to rack up medals and victories in all three sports at the local and national levels. And, don't get me started on snowshoeing. Although now retired from the competitive aspects of that wintry exercise, I have four gold medals in international snowshoe sprint racing in the Supermaster's Division. Thank you, Mr. K., for maliciously downplaying my sporty attributes as a youth in your gym classes. And, thank you for not selecting me for JV basketball in seventh grade when it was apparent that there were worse players that made the team. Your blatant disregard for talent starring you straight in the face was your problem but it nonetheless caused me to question my capabilities. Thusly, I sucked it up, stuck it out and doubled down on myself to athletically succeed at all cost in the future. So perhaps you did me a favor all those years ago because I am still competing at a high level and winning, in my elderly age group, of course. Thank you, I think.

65

That Damn Duffle Bag

I realized that my attitude and demeanor were piss poor in that class. I knew it and Mr. J.G., the eighth-grade American History teacher, knew it. I hated that class and him as well, but I really don't know why because I enjoyed learning historical factoids about the U.S.A. After all, Chester A. Arthur and George Washington were unknowing mentors for many young and impressionable boys, including me. Not to mention inspirational American political giants like Abraham Lincoln and Calvin Coolidge. So why the disgust and ambivalence shown by me in that history course? I should have loved it, absorbed it and received high marks for my efforts. But it didn't happen. From day one the instructor didn't take a liking to me and I acutely felt his bias and favoritism for "real Americans" in his classroom, not for a brown-skinned *foreigner* whose last name he repeatedly jumbled up. However, I had become used to this particular paradigm since kindergarten and usually took it in stride. There were many instances of micro-aggressions against me, but I soldiered on and grew a thick skin. But that Mr. J.G. genuinely rankled me. He smiled at the pretty girls walking

238

into his room and bantered baseball with the future "white" jocks who sat in the back. He was a stout, former jock-ass himself who also coached cross-country, junior-varsity and varsity baseball. He was an all-American kid at heart and it showed in his demeanor and treatment of his students. He just scoffed at and wrote me off early in the year as a misfit and never sought to engage me. I was cool with that. Whatever. I was still getting very decent grades in the class, even though I despised being there and "taught" by him. But then it happened: the duffle bag incident. Every year the school's athletic department would pass out certain logoed items to denote a student's participation in a varsity sport. Jackets, letters, ties, cuff links, etc. were meted out to help delineate the alpha male "winners" from the beta "losers" in our sports crazy high school culture. The varsity girl players also received "stuff" but I'm not sure if I ever noticed any of their badges or sporty tokens on display. Our *hot* cadre of cheerleaders, the same girls that cheered for football and basketball, ALWAYS had something on display, however. Anyway, in 1973 all the varsity sportsmen received complimentary duffle bags, complete with the school's colors and bulldog motif emblazoned on both sides. Oh, it was a handsome bag, I tell you. What was not to like? And guess what? I got one too! But how? It seems that there were a few extra bags left over after the 9-12 superstars got theirs. And being somewhat of a local tennis prodigy-in-the-making, the varsity men's tennis coach saw to it that I received one as well, kind of like a bribe to make sure that I joined the high school team and not just play with my old man and his college players the following spring. My father doubled as a civil engineering professor and coach for the local NJCAA college tennis team, which was usually highly ranked year after year. Since age nine, every spring found me as the after-school tagalong ball boy, glorified scut-monkey and "assistant" to my pop as he coached his athletes. On occasion I was allowed to hit with the college men, as well as receive on-court instruction from pops during actual practices! It was thrilling to be accepted and taught by players much older than me. I was getting better in a hurry and my high school tennis coach knew it. So now I had an official high school athletic department-sanctioned varsity sport duffle bag! But I made a big mistake. I should have known better but maybe my seething dislike of Mr. J.G. made me do it. I was so proud of that rumpled bag as a status symbol that I immediately started to carry it around with me from class to class, to hold my books in, and to show off a little. I wasn't a varsity stud yet and here I was sporting a "valued" piece of manly machismo as an eighth-grader. Maybe some of those cheerleader girls would give me a second look? Maybe? No dice; the only one that gave me a look, albeit a puzzled and angry one, was Mr. J.G. He didn't notice it at first because I always had the bag tucked away under my seat, but one day he spied it and went nuts. Not only was I a *putz* in his book and a wussy tennis player, but I wasn't even in ninth grade yet. Holy hell. It just didn't sit well with him. "Mayputz!" he slurred on that fateful day, "Why do YOU of all people have a varsity bag? Did you steal it? What is wrong with you? Are you an idiot? They are reserved for varsity athletes only, not TENNIS players in junior high! It's an insult to REAL varsity athletes." Well, we both turned beet red; he in rage, and me in horror and embarrassment. Most of the kids in my class hadn't even noticed that baggy accoutrement of mine until he brought it up. Now everyone knew, at least in that history classroom. Kids stared at me in amazement as I proceeded to mumble back to Mr. J.G. that Mr. P., the varsity tennis coach, had in fact given it to me. Mr. J.G. adjusted his always broken glasses, pushed them up his nose, grabbed the bag out from under my seat and started strutting around, lecturing the stunned and silent class on my arrogance and alleged misbehavior. It went on for at least five minutes before he threw the bag back at me and said that there was a grave miscarriage of justice and he never wanted to see it in his class again. I just sat there, hopelessly looking for a hole to crawl into. I never brought that bag into school again; my mother still has it, stowed away in my old bedroom closet, in mint condition. But why did he go off on me so virulently? I had heard that besides coaching he was secretly tutoring many rising baseball players on the side and never considered tennis a real sport, and here I was flaunting it in his face. Perhaps that and his already powerful disdain for me made him explode that day? I don't know. We never made up, and things continued to sour between us. My grades in his class suddenly began to suffer and tank because he started grading all my essay test questions meticulously and with malice. Before he would just glance at my writing and check it off. Now he took every chance to downgrade me if possible and left many obtuse and hurtful comments in red ink in the margins on the test packets. I could *feel* his hostility toward me. But I couldn't complain; it was his class, his examinations and his grading methodology. But my GPA in his class had slipped to a low B average and my parents were not pleased. But during a succeeding parent-teacher conference, the daring bully became the bullied. My father told me that Mr. J.G. expressed shock and frustration at my poor attitude in his class and "faulty," sarcastic, answers on many test questions that gave him no choice but to grade accordingly. As a college professor and fellow educator, my pop bought his bullcrap and admonished me for my shortcomings in American History. Oh, boy; and all because of that fuckin' maroon duffle bag. The year ended with my average in the dumpster instead of in the high A range and left me wishing for a "better" social studies experience in ninth grade. Mr. J.G. was an ass to me and I didn't appreciate it. He can take a baseball and shove it up his …. No other words need to be said. Of course, I am a lifelong Yankee's fan. Maybe I should have mentioned that to him in '72-'73? Perhaps I would have ended up with an easy-breezy A average in his class? Probably. It was all my fault. Live and learn.

66

A New Standard

As stated in the previous messed up story, I struggled in eighth grade American History class with that dastardly and ineffectual teacher Mr. J.G. Of course I didn't make it any easier on myself because of my negative attitude and ambivalence. Our mutual dislike for one another was palpable and continued throughout the school year, although there was a break in our "cold war" when the new student teacher arrived in that class. Holy moly she was pretty, and elegant, and stylish too. Va-va-voom! What a looker. Puberty already had most of us *boyz* in hormonal knots, and then she came along…. Her feminine magnetism and sexiness hit most of us dirty dogs right between the eyes. Mr. J.G. let her at us and she delivered. A gifted speaker with an ability to teach history at an understandable level, she quickly gained our trust and most students reciprocated by showing enthusiasm in class and garnering top grades during her brief but profound term. At least I did. It was a most welcome change for me. Out with the asshole and in with a hottie. But her time with us was short. Six weeks of student teaching and she was gone; back to get her college degree, teaching certificate, and then to start lecturing as an official teacher, somewhere. However, she had set a new STANDARD of teaching excellence and beauty for our *corn-fed* school, which was filled with dumpy and mostly *fugly* teachers, both male and female. However, the home economics teacher was also eye candy, but only the girls had her for an instructress, darn it. Anyway, Miss S. left us, but a curious thing had occurred. It seems that during her fleeting interlude in our esteemed (yeah, right) school she had caught the eye of our young and most handsome seventh grade New York State History teacher, Mr. K.; the same dude I had the year before. He was the same universally beloved bloke that my whole seventh grade class had adored and respected; the same fellow that ran the popular afterschool Yorker Club, of which I was then a member. There was many a time when my simpleton pals and I would joke out loud that Miss S. and Mr. K. should date. Ha, ha. And they did, behind our backs of course. And it worked out, it seems. I recently spoke to a long retired Mr. K. and his also retired, lovely wife, the former Miss S. What a love story. I love it.

67

The "Gang's" Formation

I had known E.G. well since third grade and continued to regularly goof around with him in study halls, music class, and during orchestral practices. However, now I also befriended another jokester named F., a pal that would remain my best friend for years to come. Strangely we became close quite quickly and profoundly. Prior to that we had never interacted or even noticed each other or cohabitated a single class together during our elementary school incarceration. Seventh-grade music, violin lessons and orchestra were the bonding agents that suddenly cemented our unlikely friendship that intimately endured past graduation and into the first two years of pharmacy college, which we both attended as roommates. J. Logg, my initially belligerent and boisterous, large, locker mate was now a close buddy too, and matter-of-factly jumped on board our expanding ship. E.G. enthusiastically vouched for another fellow that lived near him; G.P. also turned out to be a good egg, slightly soft boiled but a good yolk, nonetheless. N.K. was a girl I had known since kindergarten; our respective fathers both taught at the same junior college in town and her mother would someday be our high school German teacher. N.K. was alright; I used to practically live on her front porch during the time my family rented different houses on Clinton Street in the late '60s. L.B. came alongside early during seventh-grade history class when we started commiserating over our sardonic views on just about everything. She was a riot and a girl too. And last but not least was P.M., a feisty female that had transferred into our grammar school a few years back. She and I clicked while in the same fourth and sixth grade classes together. So what did us eight, cynical, smart alecks have in common? Why, an ounce of brain, humor, sarcasm, a biting wit, and the ability to laugh at ourselves as well as others. Were we the funniest kids in junior high? Maybe, maybe not. And did we mischievous monkeys solely hang out with each other? Not at all. We had other acquaintances, as needed. However, we eight wisenheimers developed a certain homing mechanism, similar to a weak magnetic field or Van der Waals forces, that kept us mentally tethered when not in close, physical proximity. On weekends we were on our own but during school hours we tried to co-mingle regularly. There was no leader of our nascent posse; we just gravitated toward each other seemingly spontaneously. We had different academic and athletic abilities along with varying familial backgrounds and values. But we found enough common ground to stick together throughout our high school tenure. Lunchtime and study halls would usually find us huddled together, chuckling and plotting amusing antics, dissecting recent TV sitcoms, and purely enjoying our camaraderie. What started as a disorganized bunch of slightly nerdy, humorous adolescents in a loose confederation morphed into a small, stalwart mob that eventually ran roughshod over our later contemporaries, teachers and administration wonks with jokes, parodies and bushwhacking bullshit. F. and I eventually took the helm of our ensemble, with me designated as the head instigator and provocateur, as we progressed to graduation. Two more male *comics* joined our group in future years, but for now, eight, zany, "gang" members were the levitous scourge of eighth grade, *and loving it*, as Maxwell Smart would say.

68

Gone Sailing

You all know the saying "gone fishing" as a metaphor for not being present, for taking a break, or for actually fishing. Well, my old man liked to fish, and many was the time when he would take our family and me to our favorite puny lake not far from our house and fish away a lazy springtime, Sunday afternoon in our lightweight, aluminum Starcraft 12-footer. He wasn't always a taskmaster, especially when he would wake me up early, dig up some earthworms in the garden and whisk us away for a father and son outing. On occasion he was genuinely great to be with. We would hurriedly untie our watercraft from the top of our '65 Oldsmobile, drop it into the drink and start paddling. As we slowly punted along the shoreline, dropping our bait lines and spinning our lures in anticipation of pickerel strikes, he would often mention sailing. Sailing? He wasn't the type or was he? Was it yet another "thing" that my dad excelled at? Hell, he could do everything else so why not sailing as well, I sarcastically thought to myself. But with what? I could not picture our dinghy as a proper sailing vessel on that dinky lake; however my father did. I sat there mesmerized as dad seriously contemplated outfitting our drab metal tub with a mast, rudder, ropes, and sail; the works! What I didn't realize is that our dowdy boat had come with a sailing package that was not bought at the time; it had the holes, spaces and mast holder already built in for a quick conversion to a mini schooner. But why did my landlubber father fancy himself an admiral, anyway? Shiver me timbers: the story is that a few years before I was born, in western New York State, pop's first civil engineering job was with an architectural firm whose owner was a wealthy and devoted yachtsman. Supposedly, his personal office was filled with nautical memorabilia and trinkets up the ying yang. He inferred sailing, he talked sailing, he lived to sail! That's what my dad said anyway. One day he asked a young, tenderfoot engineer to go for a sail in his expensive, thirty-foot, teak beauty on Lake Erie. How could pop say no? When the boss beckons, you go. You know how it is. Well, the jaunt was thrilling although not without a bout of seasickness, which was normal for someone who had never been on the roiling waves of a large lake on a windy day. But I guess my father only internalized the positive, sublime memories of that long ago watery debut and held on to that magical time all these years later. However, he couldn't begin to afford a luxurious sailing yacht on a professor's meager salary, so he schemed to convert our little skiff into his dreamboat. So he finally bought the proper accoutrements and life preservers, had us board the newly outfitted and retrofitted, glorified rowboat, and we four family members set sail. All hands on deck, please. And what a sight it was: the "captain" barking out orders to a useless and crowded crew of scared sailors, who didn't know portside from starboard as the riparian adventure soured into a head bonking misadventure. We stunk as worthy seamen and my quick-tempered father quickly booted my mom and sis from the poop deck. That swiveling boom had done them in and they were more than happy to quit. I became the quivering first mate as the old man handled the tiller like a pro and we eventually started to navigate our small body of water with ease and grace. We sailed like paupers on a glorified canoe, but, hey…. I believe in my father's head he was at the helm of his former employer's gorgeous wooden sailboat that still stuck in his mind as something worthwhile to aspire to, something to measure success with, something to be proud of. As we disembarked to go home after a typical day of brisk sailing, pop would often sigh. I didn't know what that meant? Was it a sigh of relief that we were still alive, was it out of satisfaction, or out of frustration that his reality was a tiny sloop instead of a mighty mahogany seaworthy masterpiece? I'll never know, and I was too embarrassed to ask, anyhow.

69

Townies vs. Techies

You would have thought that it might be a continuously raging war, or at least a skirmish of some sorts, but it wasn't. As harped on before, many of the townsfolk were victims of their surroundings and upbringing, including the "down to dirt" boys and girls raised on dairy farms. And the rural high school on the hill was fully "dysfunctional" with a certain agricultural flavor imbedded in its earthy fiber. Contrast that to the two-year Ag and Tech college up on the other hill in town. Approximately three thousand students, mostly from downstate New York, descended yearly on our "backward" village. Many wore trendy clothing with hairstyles to match. How did I know so much about the college? Well, both my parents retired from there as full professors, after lengthy teaching careers. I had spent oodles of hours at that place, either spectating the wrestling matches and basketball games, viewing films at MacDonald Hall inside The Little Theatre, or just visiting mom and dad at their respective offices. During the late '60s, while most *home boyz* at the high school sported crew cuts and dressed in hunting jackets, many male students at Tech were already radicalized, longhaired, hippie freaks. They had sit-ins, Vietnam War protest marches, and incessantly argued politics with conservative professors such as my old man, while concurrently learning engineering principles from him. They kept him on his toes, so he said. So there was this dichotomy of thought and appearances between the high school and college students, separated by a valley, a wide stream and the village. Nevertheless, four things may have prevented possible animosity between the two disparate groups of kids in town that were thrown together every fall. Firstly, many high school graduates attended the local college and kind of instantly blended into the fabric of collegiate life. Most commuted from home or co-rented apartments with non local students. Secondly, although the drinking age was eighteen, our town was *dry* at the time. That's right, we had no bars to get liquored up in and then start brawling. By the time the village got *wet*, in the late '70s, the polarizing political headwinds and nationwide angst had largely dissipated; people started to care more about drugs and disco than about communism and capitalism. Thirdly, Tech was known as a "suitcase" college. On most weekends the college was bereft of life as students got into automobiles and drove to their respective parental homes. The multiple parking lots were extensive and packed during weekdays but vacant on Saturdays and Sundays.

Any deleterious interaction between townies and techies was thwarted by lack of possible combatants. And, lastly, lots of the farm folk in our agricultural area were employed by the college, at least on a part-time basis. Though not necessarily professors, many received valuable bennies, such as health insurance and pensions by being custodians, secretaries, groundskeepers, dormitory directors, etc. So even though an annual autumnal chasm seemed to exist between the two different "breeds" in town, everyone ended up coexisting rather peacefully by amalgamating together. Was it ultimately because of maturity, the intermingling of minds between locals and *foreigners*, or because the growing influence and prevalence of reefer kept things peaceful? What started as a trickle became a torrent in the early '70s as Mary Jane easily climbed down the college hill, crossed the river and scaled the other hill to *stone* willing high schoolers. However, it wasn't the scourge or pandemic that our vigilant principal made it out to be. There were plenty of boys like me that witnessed contraband but never tasted or inhaled any hooch or hemp, respectively. But we were not the battling kind of kids anyway, so no worries there. Perhaps that was the fifth and real reason why potential fighting never broke out between the scurrilous native villagers and whacked out collegians. Perhaps marijuana induced widespread placidity, and an evolving *cool* culture inadvertently cooled down any would-be adversaries in town? Maybe.

70

Fixtures

Fixtures is an all-purpose word describing furniture, appliances, bathroom and kitchen faucets, tubs and showerheads, longtime business locations, and even "immovable" old codgers. What a useful word. After moving into our brand new house, which we basically built as a family of conscripted carpenters, my father continued to put the finishing touches on his architectural and engineering masterpiece. He had designed and built it, now it was time to fine tune it. You know, put railings on the back porch, pour some concrete walkways, put cabinets and lights in the upstairs bathroom, finish the cellar, etc. Little stuff, but nonetheless important for modern human habitation. And what better place was there to buy the missing links and odds and ends from? Why, from one of the oldest fixtures in town: Tuppens Brothers Hardware store on Main Street, the same one that is still there but under new ownership, and a true vintage vestige of yesteryear. It's the store that has more shit displayed in its huge front glass windows than most equivalent emporiums have in their entire stock. Yeah, that one: the original family owned hardware, plumbing and propane gas outfit

that somehow ran amok and got supersized over the years
to become a huge general store. Some businesses make it
by becoming specialized; some by generalizing and
undercutting the competition. Although in our puny
village, there was no other competition! Anyway, many was
the Saturday when my old man and I would walk down
our hill to patronize old man Tuppens and walk away with
copper pipes, screws, washers, doorknobs, etc. It wasn't
often but sometimes a Tuppens relation came to our house
and, under my dad's tutelage, would accomplish some mild
plumbing. The other plumber in town, Bob R., was not
trusted by pop after a fiasco involving almost cutting
through a house-supporting joist to make room for a
furnace duct. Anyhow, there were other fixtures in town as
well. The Mobil gas station, for instance. It was on the
corner of Main and Kingston streets and remains there
today. Pop would always get angry and argue with the
full-service attendant about the constantly rising prices in
the early '70s. However, gasoline cost less than 60 cents per
gallon of regular and the owner knew that my father was a
diehard Mobil fan who wouldn't leave him for Gulf down
the street at Maxie's. So even though pop bickered, he paid
up, and swore all the way home! I could go on and on
about the other famous and infamous village
establishments such as Dewart's Department Store, The

"Bumfuck" Motor Company, Bickham's Garage, Otter's Barber Shop, Western Auto, The Greasy Spoon, the newly defunct Smalley's Theatre, the soon to be razed bowling alley, and the local candy shop, which doubled as a meeting place for townies and techies alike. That is, if the Greek owner was in good spirits and didn't kick everyone out on a maddening whim, which was often. But I won't go on; I don't wish to bore you most intellectual readers with soporific sentimentality. To end this little ditty about fixtures, how about my blind neighbor that sold ice cream out of his pushcart downtown? He was no doubt a fixture in his own right, giving the local populace solace with his Rain or Shine perseverance and lastingness. However, one can look up the main street in almost any small settlement and be rewarded with historically nauseating nostalgia in addition to tales of longevity from tenacious tenants and proprietors. Anyhow, back in our day, my family and I just went about our business, not mindfully living in the moment or mentally luxuriating in the surroundings that one day might become important relics. For instance, one day we needed a goddamn toilet seat. My younger sister had seriously and indelibly crapped up ours, so dad and I headed to Tuppens Brothers to purchase the required part, where else? Pop wanted to *platz* on a clean crapper, and for a sawbuck got his wish.

71

I'm Not Liberace!

Much to my mother's and piano teacher's distress, I was not on course to be the next Van Cliburn, Bach, Chopin, Czerny, or even Liberace. I was good, but not that good. Actually, I was middling at best, if not worst. I was always preparing for the next recital, the next NYSSMA competition, the next performance…. My "expert" playing should have given my swollen musical ego enough comfort but it did not. Although now able to read and rehearse difficult pieces while practicing daily, the "feeling" was just not there anymore. I arrived at a crossroads of sorts in my young career as a pianist. I wanted to continue to impress my various audiences and depress those keys with skill and abandon; however my limited talent told me otherwise. I had just completed my fourth and final NYSSMA adjudication extravaganza and received an overall A for my efforts, at a Grade IV level. It was my fourth perfect score in four consecutive years. I should have been elated but was not. I dejectedly informed my teacher that I would no longer participate in the competitive rat race, much to her dismay. And that was it. I sporadically continued to play around town in different venues, eventually reaching Grade

V music while taking weekly instructions from the same instructress. But my heart wasn't in it anymore. Fast forwarding a few years found me with a different teacher, playing modern tunes, and enjoying those ivories a little more. However, a little was not enough. Before my senior year started, I had quit formal lessons altogether and played for fun only. Wasn't that why I signed up for lessons in the first place all those many years and payments ago? Not possessing the inborn musicianship required to make it in the music world was cruel gruel to swallow, no matter my determination or amount of pounding on those black and whites. It was an unfortunately realistic but sad ending for the local "piano man." Mom was disappointed and dad was ambivalent as I reluctantly gave up a "career" that I never really had, nor wanted. Was it just sour grapes? Maybe so.

72

Malevolent Music

I had breezed through the quarter of mandatory music in seventh grade so I assumed the same would happen in the quarter of eighth grade music, as well. It had the same whacked out, far out and spaced out vocal teacher, Miss R., and the same misbehaving junior high munchkins as the prior year. Miss R., my mom and I were good pals outside of class; I thought that merely showing up to her reprehensible class during eighth period was going to be a perfunctory exercise in achieving another easy A, much like last year. Well, my hubris and musical ego almost mussed up my GPA and ruined the seemingly ironclad friendship I had with her. Things started out smoothly, with me eventually signing up for another operetta called *H.M.S. Pinafore* while sitting in my usual seat in the back row with my rowdy buddies, including E.G. and F. And as usual, Miss R. started each class with a withering attack on us halfwits, calling us names for behaving so poorly, inconsiderately, and being so immature. I was thirteen years old. When could I be immature if not then? Huh? Anyway, as opposed to seventh grade, this year she warned us that all class notes would be collected for her review on top of a due project, prior to our final grades being tallied. Classroom participation and favoritism were no longer good enough for that easy A grade. I listened, closed my notebook and blatantly disregarded her frequent warnings. I thought I was untouchable, one of her "chosen few." I was so wrong. Only one of my close chums was taking notes on a regular basis and I laughed at him daily. He was a bonehead. How could he respect such a blowhard teacher when I barely did? Then a week before the project was due, I reluctantly got creative and busy. I took a box, lined it with red felt, and made a few miniscule musical instrument replicas out of pipe cleaners and haphazardly threw them in it. I didn't care because I thought she didn't either. But then, when I saw the elaborate and artistic products other students brought in, I suddenly felt that facile A slipping away. And when that *fiend* of mine, not friend, showed me the copious and detailed notes he had transcribed from her tiny blackboard hieroglyphics, I really started to worry. I only had one page of gibberish written in my notebook when I laid it on her piano as I exited that den of musical debauchery. I was screwed. What started out as a play period for me turned into a nightmare in a hurry. My other buddies didn't care; they would settle for a B or a C and move on with life. A quarterly course was not worth much and wouldn't wreck a stellar scholastic average. But it was

different with me. It was the principle of the thing. I had
willingly made my life unnecessarily hard and was
embarrassed at my futile efforts. What would she say to
me, or my mom? I didn't have to wait long for an answer.
There was one day of music class left before the quarter
ended; I came home as usual, and got an earful from my
mother. She went on and on about how Miss R. couldn't
understand why a stellar student and good boy like me had
gone ahead and become a CLOWN who deserved nothing
higher than a C. That hurt. I mean, I knew I WAS one, but
I didn't appreciate being called one, not to my face anyway.
And the C was not acceptable, period. However, mom said
that I could rectify the sordid situation in the following
way: Miss R. would reaccept a BETTER project from me
that COULD significantly raise my grade. That night I
basically copied my previous effort, but this time used my
extensive toy model-making know-how and artistic talent
to cut, glue, pose and finish a mini masterpiece. The end
result consisted of a red, felt-lined box, twenty puny pipe
cleaner musicians holding various musical instruments
made out of shiny gold paper, all glued firmly to the
bottom, resembling an orchestral setup, complete with a
conductor on a rostrum. I stayed up until 2 a.m., with my
father poking his head in my lit up room during a
nighttime bathroom break and wondering why I was up so

late. I told him and he just shook his head in disbelief. I handed in my magnum opus in the morning, so Miss R. could grade it before our class period in the afternoon. She gingerly accepted it and smiled. I cowered and stammered something as I left her classroom and hoped that it would be enough for an A. It was report card day as we handed her our report cards during that last period of the day to have her mark our final grades in it. I received a low A, much to the amazement of my immediate cohorts. I didn't say a word and neither did Miss R. I had learned a valuable lesson and realized that I could easily have been punished for my arrogance, negativity and endless joking around. But Miss R. had given me a break, a friendly bounce, a liberal line call and I really appreciated it. Throughout the rest of my future schooling, including colleges, which was extensive, exhausting and often difficult, I never ever came to class unprepared or purposely pompous. I checked my attitude at the door and then proceeded to do my best. Thanks, Miss R. for believing in me and giving me a second chance. Lesson learned.

An Old Hand

Makeup, please! Then cold cream, to take it off! I had voluntary signed on to my first school operetta as a seventh grader and loved the experience, except for all the bellyaching students and the deranged, loudmouthed director, Miss R. She was the junior high music/vocal teacher with the big, blonde, bouffant hairdo, and the de facto producer/director of the yearly faux operatic production. Yeah, we knew each other well, both inside and outside the classroom. Her elderly father was my entomological mentor, his dogs were my "summer" pets, and my mom and she would regularly *kibbitz* when running into each other on Clinton Street, my former place of residence. So it was a no-brainer for me to step forward as a neophyte seventh grader in her derelict music class and get her approval for a non vocal role in the upcoming spectacle. She had expected me to be in it and I didn't disappoint. I had been in so many piano performances over the years that I felt ready for the "big stage," if only in a small, insignificant, non singing role. And I had a blast. We performed *Tom Sawyer* in 1972, with me playing one of Huck Finn's weasely friends. I had many group scenes, a few solo outings and scant dialogue; just the way I liked it. There were a few other 12-year-olds in my midst, but we were overshadowed by older students that could really act and sing at the same time. We weren't maligned, just had to know our subordinate places and be respectful of Miss R. and the real stars of the show. However, the many afterschool and evening practices drove Miss R. crazy, if that was possible. No shows, latecomers, missed lines, stage fright, etc. all combined to make the rehearsals a mind-blowing and nervous experience for all involved. Miss R. was screeching, the lighting people didn't know a spotlight from a stoplight, the lead actor (Tom Sawyer) was sick and barfing on stage, and Huck was just sitting there cross-legged, and stoned out of his mind. And that was during a good practice. I took it all in and loved it. Nevertheless, we made it to the dress rehearsal and nailed it. The resulting product was smooth and professional, with much commendation from the parents, teachers and administration in attendance in our gorgeous, old-fashioned auditorium. In 1973 the operetta was *H.M.S. Pinafore*, a Gilbert and Sullivan comedic send-up about the shenanigans aboard a ship involving the captain, his lovely daughter and her love for a lowly sailor. As an "old hand" at this "acting" game by now, and after the previous year's success, I again volunteered to be part of the whacky ensemble. Miss R. was thrilled and once again I scored a speaking part only, and got ready for action. It felt good bossing around the anxious seventh graders and to give them tips on where to stand, how to properly enunciate, elocute, and how to adroitly enter and exit. The prep work followed the same arc as the previous extravaganza I was in. The same harried practice sessions, the same flustered and bedeviled musical director at the forefront and mostly the same lame students that always got the job done at the eleventh hour. Miss R. was always visibly apoplectic and profusely sweating during our time together and we would-be thespians strangely delighted in that. Hmm.... Anyhow, we rehearsed, we performed, and we took our bows. However, I was finished. I never again participated in another school operetta or dramatic play, for that matter. I'm not sure why, though. Although high school found me onstage numerous times, whether performing on the piano, in the varsity choir, orchestral recitals, doing the stage lighting with F., or in original sketch comedies with my own troupe as warm-up acts, Miss R. and I did not cross paths again while in school. Twice was enough. No more school sanctioned singing baloney for me. But it was great while it lasted.

74

Whatever Happened to Dusty?

He was the Fonz in sixth grade, at least in my classroom. Popular, smart, relaxed, charming and athletic, he was a teacher's dream student, while the rest of we dorky dimwits just sat there like dumpy dumps. Although just a tad fluffy for his age, he nonetheless possessed confidence and maturity that was way beyond his tender years, as well as a primordial mustache. As an interbred local, he was friends with everyone, including that sometimes obnoxious wise cracker and sporty jerk named N.Z., who was a real "character," even back then. F.D.'s nickname was Dusty, and he had even helped ME out one day by beating back a bully, with a little assistance from a few other pals of mine. He was a good fellow. By seventh grade he had secured the vice-presidency of our class and was a valued member of the junior high football and wrestling teams. That guy was going places, we all said. He also had an easy rapport with the ladies; I was so envious of him! Although I was a perceived intellectual and rising athlete, Dusty had the *swag* and *rep* all locked up for twelve-year-old boys in our seventh grade. However, by the end of eighth grade, the luster and brilliant potential that was Dusty had largely worn off. My friends and I barely spoke to him in the hallways and did not have him in any of our classes together. He seemed to have become lost in the shuffle of junior high and no longer had a captive audience to preside over. His big bid at "stardom" seemed to have ended the year before. He had reached dizzying heights and the pinnacle of his student tenure at an early age and seemingly could not keep it going; he had fizzled out. At least that's what the rest of my buds and I sarcastically inferred. Maybe he had it coming to him? Perhaps he had started up with a bad crowd? But for whatever reason, he effectively "disappeared" from our grade while some of us goofballs, including myself, rose up to dominate the class in wisdom, wit, sports and the arts. I vaguely remember him at senior graduation, still a bit pudgy but without the bluster and bravado he used to exude in spades. He looked crestfallen, spent, adrift, and definitely not top college material while most of my friends and I were just "chomping at the bit" to get the hell out of high school, hit higher education and make our indelible marks in the world. Was this a cautionary tale and a little karmic justice, or both or neither? Perhaps it was all by choice and we simply grew up into our own lives while outgrowing him? Still, we all graduated, but whatever happened to Dusty?

75

ZotZ

His *idiot-syncrasies*, affectations and mannerisms made him a slightly strange man. Perhaps his inner demons or frustrations at only being a junior high school art teacher contributed to his temperamental, esoteric, and eclectic behavior. Or, perhaps, maybe he was just slightly strange…. He wasn't that bad but vastly different from Mr. G., our staid grammar instructor, for instance. Mr. L. and I had this artful love-hate relationship going on. I had more than an ounce of talent and LOVED to draw and paint; he mostly HATED my shit and had told me so daily during our quarter together the previous year. I'm not sure if he was goading me into becoming better or just used me as a classic whipping boy for his own prurient pleasure. Nonetheless, he gave me an A in seventh grade and sarcastically said he looked forward to working with me again in eighth. Did he say working with me or working me over? What was wrong with him? He had gotten under my skin and he knew it, routinely needling me and my creative endeavors. Oh, well, there was only a month left in the quarter and then junior high art would be over with, once and for all! Actually, the whole school year would be over with, too. Thank goodness! Then one day while Mr. L. was holding court at the front of the class, and before letting us dunces loose on clay modeling, a male student (most probably that insufferable *eccentric*, N.Z.) from the back of the expansive room got his attention and threw him a small, cellophane wrapped object. Ordinarily, Mr. L. would not have appreciated an interruption of his artistic sermon by us bozos; however, this time candy was involved. He caught the tiny projectile flying at him, studied it carefully, looked back at the snickering student, unwrapped it, and popped the contents into his mouth! "ZotZ," he proclaimed loudly, as a few knowing pupils erupted in laughter. Mr. L.'s eyes popped out as he repeated that "Z" name over and over again, while chewing and laughing. What the hell was going on? I had never heard of that confection before. What was it and what made Mr. L. so jovial all of a sudden? Well, it was a hard candy with an interior of bicarbonate of soda and tartaric acid that when bitten into mixed the two chemicals together, causing a fizzing sensation and foaming at the mouth, if left open. It was a sweet and sour oral sensation that had gotten the best of Mr. L. I eventually ate some myself and didn't think it was an earth shattering experience. Obviously, he thought otherwise. Anyway, that quick intervention by that certain student seemed to have abruptly changed the tone of the class. Somehow Mr. L. lightened up and stopped being such an annoying *nudge*, at least to me. And he kept asking for more ZotZ whenever we entered his enlarged second floor studio for class. Other students now knew his "weakness" and provided him with those sour, tasty treats as if giving him a fix of an illicit drug. The rest of that quarter quickly dissipated and we finished that artsy fartsy class, with kilns afire and last minute projects getting graded. Surprisingly and much to my relief, I scored an A once more in a course that I simultaneously adored and despised. That left my bruised and bloated artistic ego relatively intact; however, did I owe much of the credit to a piece of bonbon? Did ZotZ really soften up Mr. L. to such an extent that he got soft in the head and forgot how much he "hated" me? I doubt it. Nevertheless, perhaps there WAS something special and magical in that little sweet. Or perhaps Mr. L. was just a weirdo and happened to enjoy "hard sugar" delights containing effervescent bangs!

76

Guidance?

Their office was next door to the Audio Visual department; you know, it's the room full of frequently malfunctioning movie projectors, tape recorders, TVs, and the outcast, malfunctional nerdy boys who set them up for the teachers. Anyway, in reality the two guidance counselors, Mr. T. and Mr. M., were our TRUE fearless leaders. They were wholly responsible for "guiding" the students in grades 7 – 12, throughout the whole junior high and high school experience. Only TWO guys in control of the destinies of over seven hundred pupils; Holy Mackerel! Mr. M. was the son of my former third grade teacher, was middle-aged, smoked unfiltered Camels like his mom, always had a ballpoint pen tucked behind his right ear, and had an affable disposition, while taking on the first half of the alphabet. Mr. T., on the other hand, was a former shop teacher in our school who rose up through the ranks to his dream job, to counsel young boys and girls about their usually bleak futures. Are you serious? He was also middle-aged, composed and with somewhat of a mean streak. He took on the latter half of the students, M through Z. I had visited Mr. T. for the first time in the fall of seventh grade

273

to make sure the courses I was in were appropriate and to check on my early progress in them. Then we had our mandatory meeting in the spring of '72, to discuss and sign up for eighth grade classes for the following fall. It had been no big deal, just perfunctory nodding and small talk on my part as I continually committed to a science and math, Regents curriculum. It was also undoubtedly painless for him to plot my adolescent future thus far. I was a relatively intelligent young lad who *seemed* to know what I wanted, where I was going and appeared to be trouble free, at least in scholastic matters. He didn't ask about my home life, my perceived prejudices against me or my mental well-being. And why should he have? Good Lord, he was a former shop teacher, not a trained school psychologist! Or, maybe he was? I knew for sure that he was also a painter, not an artist, but a house painter. He and my future math teacher had a bustling side hustle going on, coloring most of the village homes. They were a well-known team and I guess did adequate work, climbing metal scaffolding and ladders and, unlike Laurel and Hardy, did not spill much paint on the ground, or on each other. Or, so I had heard. Anyway, it was time for my second compulsory eighth grade confessional with Mr. T. After planning out my course selections for ninth grade next fall, I left his office that rainy spring day in 1973 and wondered what he did the rest of the year while at his day job. I mean, he had only seen me four times in two years. His profession must be a joke, I mistakenly thought. Only later, during conversations with outlier acquaintances, did it finally sink in that he and Mr. M. were indeed the de facto school psychologists and, besides discussing whether a student should take study hall instead of art, had a line of misbehaving, obstinate, and scurvy guys and gals to deal with on a daily basis. But were they trained in such matters? Who knew? And what about suicide prevention, smoking cessation and treating reefer madness? Yes, they did that too. Wow, I started to gain new respect for those two clowns as I thought about THEIR credentials and career choices. And I started to pity the fools that had to see Mr. T. for academic indiscretions because although a scrawny bloke, he had a quick temper and was not easily bamboozled. Nevertheless, I would see him more times in the future as he effortlessly *guided* me until graduation.

Specs

Although born and bred in this country, I was constantly fighting the "foreigner" stigma. Being brown complexioned, brown-eyed and black-haired, and having immigrant parents already made me unattractive to the "albino" *home gurls* in my adopted village; wearing glasses would just be the nail in the coffin. I was diagnosed in third grade as myopic and was prescribed corrective lenses. However, like a *schmuck*, I didn't wear them all the time. I took them on and off as needed and sneakily scuttled those spectacles during gym class and when on the bus. I squinted and faked it through seventh grade but by the end of eighth, I had those romance-killers wrapped firmly around my head. My long distance eyesight was failing and I had to wear them, even in Phys Ed, at the cost of possibly breaking them. My mother was nearsighted and religiously wore her horn-rimmed glasses; she greatly sympathized with my plight. Pop was perfect you know, and shook his head dejectedly at yet another failing of mine. He did however have the wisdom to have me outfitted with metal frames and state-of-the-art plastic lenses, and that alone saved him hundreds of dollars over the years in repairs. Not that I abused them or was willfully negligent or derelict. I never sat on my glasses or let others wear them. Nevertheless, by the completion of eighth grade they were firmly embedded on my face, and at that point I didn't really care what the girls thought of me. I needed to see, dammit. I had my newly formed group of like-minded, comically-enhanced friends and soldiered on through life. And it was interesting to see others, even attractive females in my class, having to use glasses too. Invisible contacts and Lasik surgery were a few years in the future; meanwhile it made me feel unburdened seeing the multitude of sexually struggling adolescents also in "pain" of having four eyes and braces on their teeth to boot.

78

The Broken Pinky

It was an unusually warm and non rainy, early spring day as I exited the back of the school building to catch a quick glimpse of some ongoing varsity tennis matches before joining my baby sister in our usual walk home. We often rode Bus 57 in the mornings but not at night. As I stood there by the fence, boringly watching our number one singles player take a beating by a visiting competitor from Sherburne-Earlville high school, and while waiting for sis to show up, I noticed an impromptu modified dodgeball game going on. Some lowly male sixth graders were using the side of the school as a backstop and taking turns chucking a worn-out volleyball at a student at the wall and counting how many throws it took to get him out. Everyone got a chance to be the hero in front of the brick facade while dodging or trying to catch that hard ball. I had developed a bit of a reputation as a hard out in dodgeball while in the elementary grades and brashly approached the underclassmen and boastfully asked for a turn at the wall. The small group acquiesced and seemed to relish the chance to hit an upperclassman, especially one that was bragging so much. However, my quick reflexes and skills kept me up there, longer than any other kid had been. Then I realized that the bunch was getting tired of tossing that tattered ball at me. But just as I was about to leave, I nonchalantly and haphazardly stuck out my left hand to catch one last fling. Ouch! The ball smashed the pinky of my left hand against the bricks and I was unanimously called out. The little cadre of boys cheered; I didn't protest as I quickly grabbed my throbbing and paralyzed pinky with my right hand and stiffly walked away, embarrassed and not wanting to show any pain. Perhaps it was karmic justice to have been punished for being such a braggadocious bastard, I thought to myself. I did not tell my sister anything as we silently loped home and she wasn't observant enough to ask me any questions. As soon as we arrived, I bolted through the front door, shucked off my shoes and book bag and made a beeline for the piano. Mom thought I was dying to play; I was dying to know if I could STILL play. I knew that my pinky was busted up badly and not just sprained, but what could I do? Tell my perfectionist father about my stupidity and give him yet another chance to loudly admonish me? I don't think so. It always appeared that he was just waiting for the chance to yell at me for something. Didn't he have his own life and shortcomings? Anyhow, I could gingerly play the piano keys and scale without wincing too much. Maybe nobody in my family or my music teacher would notice? Fast forward a few months, long after the searing pain and numbness had abated: my mother noticed an obvious bump on my pinky at the first knuckle location. She grabbed my hand and examined it carefully while waiting for me to enlighten her about my unfortunate misadventure. I spilled the beans and then told her that it was still usable, but I could not bend it toward my palm any longer. Well, she dutifully told my father, who went haywire as expected. His "disappointing and delinquent" son had done it again; this time mangling his hand without telling his parents about it. However, after a few "cooling off hours," pop took me to our local hospital emergency room to visit the one and only Dr. C., a gifted Korean general surgeon, who belonged in a financially lucrative suburban clinic and not in our "chicken and eggs" town. He took one look, took one x-ray, and took off to another room. His blasé assistant had to break the bad news to my dad and me that my fractured finger had healed incorrectly and needed to be rebroken and pinned together for a positive result. I had waited too long to seek easy medical treatment such as aspirin analgesia and simple splint therapy. I had stubbornly and quietly quaked in agony, not wanting to antagonize my temperamental father. And without that additional surgery, the unsightly calcified

bump would be a lifetime reminder of my fearful idiocy.
Well….I still have that hardened lump on my little finger.

79

Up to Speed

I was slowly finishing up the troublesome and unrewarding eighth grade, my dad would shortly be leaving for his last summer of master's schooling at RIT, and I would once again be left to my own devices. Tennis, pool time, helping around the house and garden, collecting newts, salamanders and insects, trying to avoid my bellicose grandpa Pete, and bike riding as often as possible were my warm weather vices and most everyone knew it. Okay, I wasn't a complete saint and never fully capitulated to dutifully remain at home as an obedient worker bee. I had not stayed put in the preceding summers, either. I just had to do my own thing, even at the risk of drawing the ire and wrath of my *old-world* paternal grandfather, who measured someone's worth by how much physical labor he did. We had a marginal truce for I had assumed more responsibilities as I grew older and shouldered many of the burdens of home repairs, etc., especially during my father's summertime absences. But sometimes I had to get away to hit some tennis balls and to hit the paved roads with my bicycle. And in May, just before the school year ended, my usually strict and demanding father miraculously bestowed upon me one of his prized possessions. No, not his scoped, Smith and Wesson 357 Magnum deer hunting pistol, and no, not his favorite Fenwick fishing pole, and no, not one of his many valuable Omega wristwatches that he had meticulously repaired over the years (he was also an expert horologist/gunsmith), but his expensive, 1959, ten-speed, Campagnolo derailleur system, racing, Raleigh two-wheeler. He had bought it the year I was born and rode it regularly until the last couple of years. It kind of sat there lonely, in the right-hand corner of our garage before he flat out told me that I could have it. "But what about my trusty, golden Schwinn?" I asked him. "We'll keep it as a backup," he cavalierly replied as he methodically checked over his now "former" pedaled steed and deemed it roadworthy to ride. The thin tires were properly inflated, the gears greased, and the brake calipers adjusted before I gingerly swung out onto our dead-end street on that magnificent blue cycle. The uncomfortable narrow seat was leather-made, the taped handlebars were curved like rams' horns, and the gears numbered ten instead of five. I had to hunch over it like a horse jockey and master a different ergonomic form of leg-powered transportation. But it was worth it. Within a few minutes I was not only a convert but felt brave enough to take off on that streak of painted metal. Many hours on weekends throughout my high school deployment were spent on that bicycle, traversing my town and the outlying hilly highways while churning and unintentionally developing my legs. And even when I had acquired a driver's permit and then license, I never needed a car; I had a bike. However in those days, no one wore any protective attire; I had no wrist guards, kneepads or helmet. Luckily, I never fell off or had any serious accidents while logging hundreds of miles on that ball-breaking seat. And fortunately there was little or light traffic in and about our town which made the cycling rather safe. Although on numerous occasions I was chased by angry, territorial, canines while passing their homely hovels, especially while coasting on barely paved back roads. Sometimes the growling and biting dogs would seemingly come out of nowhere and startle me. My heart rate was already through the roof from hard peddling, I didn't need more aggravation from those dumb animals. So I started *packing* a small wooden baseball bat, securely attached next to my water bottle, just in case of toothy trouble. I pedaled and swung my bat as needed at the heel-nipping hounds while enjoying the expansive vistas I trekked through. By the way, I never bonked any mutts on their bony heads, and most left me alone after finally recognizing me as that recurring speedy interloper and not a threat. For a nervous adolescent leading a relatively structured and conservative home life, being able to physically extricate myself from my depressing domicile to have a few hours of unbridled freedom was most exhilarating and probably therapeutic. Perhaps it was the endorphin release, the mental peace I experienced, or the beautiful rush of the surroundings, but whatever it was, I entered "the zone" whenever biking around and was forever grateful to my old man for his gift to me.

80

Jarts and Friends

Our annual end of summer, Connecticut, beachside, camping adventure had the obligatory family bonding experience as well as the usual brush with tons of other campers, seafood, biking, swimming, fishing, sun, fun, and jellyfish stings. However, there was one more oddity on display at that huge campground: youngsters and oldsters alike participating in sports, pseudosports and games that they probably would not engage in at home; namely, horseshoes, Hula-Hooping, Frisbee tossing, flag football, coed softball, and playing jarts. Jarts? You know, lawn darts, those footlong plastic flights with the heavy, sharpened steel points on the end that you threw underhand at a circle about thirty feet away, and then dodged the oncoming barrage of the same "missiles" from the opposing team to the circle on your side. That skill game, remember? The one that was finally completely eradicated from the market in 1988 after thousands of injuries and a few deaths; that game. Kind of like cornhole but with pointed objects and potentially deadly consequences. But back in the day we played it nonchalantly and with nary a worry in the world. We also played flag football without mouth guards, rode our bikes without helmets, and didn't slather on antibacterial soap/alcohol from disinfectant dispensers throughout the day. Most of us lived, too. I'm not being flippant or glib but those carefree youthful days spent camping were often filled with "dangerous" activities that even young-at-heart adults took pleasure in! Usually there was no one to blame but ourselves if trouble befell us. However, I strongly believe that even as kids we had an innate sense of personal responsibility that is most likely sorely lacking in today's younger generation. Either that or we were just recklessly lucky.

I thought this vignette would suffice as an appropriate ending to this book. By now you all know the gists of what most of my junior high experiences were like, as well as taken a peek at my stressful home life. Although there were a few peaceful and happy interludes, my days and nights were often dysfunctional, irrational, bumbling, humbling and full of flux and angst. Fortunately my developing sense of humor and good friends managed to get me through the toughest of those times. The above title is a slightly unintentional paradox and ironically describes that volatile

'70s era: the Vietnam War, smog, puberty, cyclamates, DDT, shag rugs, bell-bottoms and playing with deadly, sharpened, dart-like spears while blissfully laughing and ignoring the danger in our very hands. Ninth grade would be up next. Would my close pals and I be ready? Maybe. Since childhood my pushy parents kept pushing me and I kept pushing myself, yet the world and life kept pushing back. WTF? Hopefully the following year and my ensuing high school tenure would change for the better. And it did, despite President Ford's stupid, 1974 WIN (Whip Inflation Now) lapel buttons and disco, which was insidiously creeping into our airwaves and dance halls. It's always something…. I still hate Donna Summer and the Bee Gees.

81

Disclaimer

I wish to "apologize" to all my former fellow junior high compadres and teachers that I may have inadvertently insulted or, even worse, slightly offended. Hopefully my comedic overtures and jibes only hit your funny bones and did not cause undo consternation, constipation or ill feelings. My intent was to expose and ridicule my own life, warts and all, with supporting players included, as needed. I'm sorry if I dragged unsolicited students and unwary educators down with me. As my fourth comedic volume in print, I hope you readers enjoyed perusing this book as much as I loved writing it. I heartily encourage everyone to revisit their seventh and eighth grade cranial cortex crannies and jot down the memories found within, both good and bad. Maybe even recall other remembrances from usually cluttered and cobwebbed noggins as well? I'm told that putting pen to paper can be fundamentally therapeutic; hopefully more fun than mental. I also find it to be a cathartic, humorous and soul-cleansing release. Perhaps you will too. And if a book comes of it, so be it. Don't be afraid; we all learned SOME grammar along the way, even me. So get ON your duff and start writing!

82

Last Words

In spite of the "odds" stacked against me, I always fought the good fight, "battling" my parents, school, the piano, gym class, teachers, and mostly myself. My folks wanted me to excel; I desired to just make it out of junior high alive with my faculties, humor and grade point average in a relatively decent state. That's all. And forget about straight A's; I settled for a low A overall GPA and was truly grateful for "escaping" seventh and eighth grades. But it was the best I could have done under the circumstances. While appearing isolated from the rest of the nation and its problems, we were in fact still connected to it. Vietnam, pot, Nixon, Red Dye No. 2, Afro Sheen, *Laugh-In*, etc. were things that greatly affected my fellow bumblers and I, even in *cow country*, because we had ready access to TVs, radios, record players, records, newspapers, print media, and the college in town. We were highly informed although perhaps remained slightly naïve at the same time. Most of us that are just barely alive today can firmly attest to those testy and turbulent times of yesteryear with a wry smile, if only as a sarcastic gesture and woeful reminder of our often-disaffected youth, overlaid by unwarranted and unwanted educational and domestic anxiety. Elementary school had seen the rise of a boy that liked to make people laugh; however, that budding comedic future was thwarted and largely left adrift in junior high, much to my dismay. I left eighth grade older but not necessarily wiser and *soberly* awaited the beginning of high school. And I hadn't even had a drink, yet.

Thanks for the read.

About the Author

Dr. I. Mayputz (not his real name) graduated with highest honors from high school, from pharmacy college and summa cum laude from dental school. After completing a master's degree in prosthodontics at a then prestigious institution, he embarked on his dental career in private practice. He once briefly toyed with the idea of earning a Ph.D. to become an actual entomologist, but ultimately decided on a dreadfully stressful albeit lucrative career instead. In addition to being an elite master's athlete, author, naturalist and part-time naturist, he is also known as a caustic wit and provocateur. He wrote this book to entertain family, friends, and any curious sod willing to mentally muddle through junior high school again.

For more alleged levity by Dr. I. Mayputz, please read:

Dental School: A Bizarre Comedy

Pharmacy College: Crazy Daze and Hazy Nites

Elementary School: Wits and Twits

WHO
DAT?